FORGETTING ENGLISH

FORGETTING ENGLISH

✧ *Stories* ✧

MIDGE RAYMOND

EASTERN WASHINGTON UNIVERSITY PRESS

14 13 12 11 10 09   5 4 3 2 1

Cover: Paul Gauguin, *The Siesta,* ca. 1892–94. Oil on canvas; 35 x 45.75 inches (88.9 x 116.2 cm). Courtesy of the Metropolitan Museum of Art, Walter H. and Leonore Annenberg Collection.
Gift of Walter H. and Leonore Annenberg, 1993; bequest of Walter H. Annenberg, 2002.
Image © The Metropolitan Museum of Art.

Cover and interior design by Christine Holbert.

Library of Congress Cataloging-in-Publication Data

Raymond, Midge.
 Forgetting English: stories / Midge Raymond.
   p. cm.
 ISBN 978-1-59766-046-4 (pbk.: alk. paper)
 I. Title.
 PS3618.A9855F67 2008
 813'.6—dc22

                    2008044546

The paper used in this publication meets the requirements of ANSI/NISO Z39.48-1992 (Permanence of Paper).

Eastern Washington University Press
Spokane and Cheney, Washington

For my family,
and in loving memory of
Dr. Kitten Keith

CONTENTS

It is not down on any map; true places never are.

—Herman Melville, *Moby-Dick*

FIRST SUNDAY

Moa

H e lives in his mother's house, with no electricity or hot water, yet somehow he always has a ready supply of condoms. The notion strikes me one night as he rolls away from me and gets out of bed. He stands in the shadows of Cheryl's bedroom, a stripe of yellow light coming through from the kitchen (my sister is fortunate enough to have electricity, though she doesn't have hot water). As the kitchen light dapples the muscles of his bare chest, I make a mental note to change the sheets before Cheryl comes home.

He looks down at me. We've learned very little about each other, and while that should have changed things between us, it hasn't. He is engaged to a woman from his village, he told me last night, but they haven't slept together and won't until the first Sunday after they are married. I told him it didn't matter. He asked if I had a *moa* back home, a boyfriend, and I said yes. I lied. I wanted things to feel equal between us.

And in a way things do feel that way, as much as they aren't. Sione is twenty-three, and the thirteen years between us makes me feel old under my pale, lived-in skin, the highlights in my hair covering its early gray. Sione's brown, hairless body is as smooth as heated caramel, and his short black hair is thick between my fingers.

The language barrier, I think, helps more than hinders. A couple of times I've practiced my newly acquired Tongan words on him, but he prefers to speak to me in English, as if to keep a distance between us.

"*Pou'li ā,* Sione," I say as he leans down to kiss me good-bye.

"Good night, Melanie," he answers, smiling. I smile back, not minding that he doesn't call me Mel, like everyone else. I like the softness of my name in his mouth. I watch the width of his body fill Cheryl's small doorway, then hear the nearly noiseless sound of his feet on the dirt road, on the way back to his mother's house.

Uma

Cheryl said she would be gone a week. It surprised me that she left right away, even though I knew my visit was sudden, unexpected, perhaps not entirely welcome. The day after I arrived, I woke alone under the leaky roof of her house. She left me fresh water and some food in the icebox, and she apparently left me in charge of a trio of mangy cats and the red pig that lives in her yard.

It's been four years since I've seen my sister, and the first thing she did when she saw me at Nuku'alofa's open-air airport was sniff my hair, or maybe it was the back of my neck. She leaned in, first to one side, then the other, inhaled, then stood back, holding my arms as a breeze swirled around us. Her wide brown eyes crumpled as they always did when she smiled, but when her skin stretched taut against the fine bones of her face I noticed how skinny she'd become. As she once told me, it wasn't easy to be a vegan living in a kingdom of pork.

"What the hell was that?" I asked, miming her greeting.

"Uma fe'iloaki," she said. "It's how Tongans greet their loved ones."

I followed her out to the truck she had borrowed from a neighbor in her village. "This is going to sound terrible," she said as we climbed in, "but I have to go to Ha'apai tomorrow. Just for a couple of days. There's a new volunteer who needs some help getting her program off the ground."

"You got out of the Peace Corps years ago," I said. "Can't someone else do it?"

"I don't mind," she said, which was typical. Cheryl never could refuse help to anyone, even at her own expense. "Besides," she added, "it'll give you a chance to rest and get over the jet lag."

The last time I saw Cheryl was Christmas, four years ago, at our parents' house in Connecticut. She was about a year into her Peace Corps contract, and she'd been in Hawai'i, on medical leave for a root canal. As a Christmas present, we flew her home for the holidays, but it wasn't a gift she wanted. She seemed to have forgotten where she came from; she muttered to herself in Tongan and ate with her fingers until she caught one of us giving her a look. Later, when she told us she wasn't coming back, I thought of Bligh's crew, the ones who'd "gone native," and I half expected to find her with piercings and tattoos, with grass skirts and a Tongan husband.

But she lives alone in a squat green house, with a leaky roof and an outhouse. She wears wraparound cotton skirts and T-shirts. She doesn't look much different; the lines in her face show the effects of the sun more than her thirty-eight years. When I called after all this time and announced my visit, she didn't flinch—same old Cheryl: open arms, no questions asked—and for that I was grateful. Still, something is different, something unseen. The night I arrived, as we sat on the wooden benches in her dim living room, I looked at her and couldn't think of a thing to say.

Palangi

I met Sione my first day here, on my way into town. Cheryl had drawn me a map and left me her bike. I hadn't gone far when I heard dogs barking, which I ignored until they drew closer. When I glanced back, I saw a pack of four lean, angry dogs lunging at the pedals, targeting my feet. I shouted and kicked at them, unaware that I was weaving my bike into the road. The sound of a car horn filled my ears, and a truck skimmed past, narrowly missing my rear wheel. The driver pulled over, a young Tongan guy, and he got out and clapped his hands and yelled at the dogs: *"'Alu mama'o!"* He made a funny noise: *chhuut.* The dogs took off, running, headed back to wherever they came from.

I dismounted, my legs shaking, and he smiled. "You're Cheryl's sister," he said, his English heavily accented.

"How'd you know that?" Then I recognized the truck—the same one Cheryl borrowed to pick me up at the airport. "You must be her neighbor," I said.

" 'Io," he said, nodding. "Where are you going? You want a ride to town?"

He lifted my bike into the back of the truck, then got in. I hopped in on the passenger's side, and, with a jerk, we were back on the road. I snuck a glance at him. His lips curved upward as he turned dark eyes on mine, as if he felt my gaze. Dust floated in through the open windows, coating my eyes and tongue.

He dropped me off at the market, and I offered to cook for him that evening, to thank him. He demurred at first but finally agreed. As I walked the narrow aisles of the cramped grocery, I reminded myself that I wasn't in New York, that this was not my normal life. Usually when I invite a man over for dinner, it's somewhere around our third date, give or take, and he always stays for breakfast. I wasn't thinking this way when I invited Sione, but as I picked up fruits and vegetables, I remembered his broad shoulders, smooth brown skin, inky black hair. I decided not to rule anything out.

He ended up leaving just before dawn, as a hint of light edged into the sky. Men, I thought, are no different, even in the farthest corners of the world.

But I've offered to cook for him again tonight, our last night together having Cheryl's house to ourselves. I can tell he doesn't like my cooking—and I can't blame him—but I feel it's a necessary pretense, something that softens the fact that he's coming over for sex.

In Cheryl's kitchen, I find some spices, an onion, and three mushy cloves of garlic. I still have some noodles and vegetables. I'm not a committed vegan, like Cheryl—I used to love to tease her by ordering steak or pork whenever we ate together—but I couldn't bring myself to buy the strange, unfamiliar meats I saw in the grocery. I did buy a very expensive Diet Coke and a bag of Twisties, so if my stir-fry doesn't turn out, Sione and I can eat those. Unless we skip eating altogether.

I return to the living room and pick up Cheryl's Tongan dictionary. I look up a few key words—hello, goodbye, bathroom—then the word for foreigner: *palangi*. I repeat it to myself several times. That's what I am now, a *palangi*.

I remember what Cheryl told me when she first joined the Peace Corps. They'd given her three locations to choose from, and she chose Tonga, she said, because it was the only place she hadn't heard of. She had to look it up on a map to be sure it existed.

I look around, as if for clues that would make her less of a stranger. But her house is empty, except for the animals and her few spindly pieces of furniture. She's always lived sparely because she likes to be mobile. She doesn't believe in getting good at one thing and taking herself to the top; she sees jobs and homes as projects, as things she'll finish and then move on. Here, she has no job anymore; she lives off her garden of vegetables and off occasional tasks she can do for money or supplies. And this dim, stuffy little house has been home for twice the time she usually spends in any one place.

'Ulungāanga kovi

Sione and I eat as we did our first night together, in Cheryl's living room with our plates on our laps. Though his English is good, he is quiet, sometimes leaving me unsure of how much he understands. We drink whiskey from chipped ceramic cups, and he tells me about working in the bush, reaping harvests of *mānioke* and *'ufi*, the root vegetables that grow from his family's soil. To make extra money, he does odd jobs around the village. I find this incredibly sexy. I can't remember the last time I went out with a man who could do more than change a light-bulb.

"And you?" he asks.

"I'm the director of marketing for the US division of a Chinese electronics company." The present tense rolls off my tongue so easily it almost makes me forget what happened. I still like the way it sounds, the confidence with which I say it. "I'm sort of taking some time off."

"Holiday?"

"It's a long story," I say. He has only picked at his food. I take our plates and put them in the sink. He follows with the cups, and in the cramped kitchen, he's very close. I put my hands on his shoulders, then outline his arms with my fingers, down to the wrists. "Thanks for coming tonight," I say. Then I lift my face to his.

He looks at me, his lips in their usual half smile, then bends his head to mine. As we kiss, I slip my arms around his neck, and he pulls me closer. I lead him to Cheryl's bedroom. He is like a teenager, infinitely passionate, only with more staying power. Every square inch of my body responds to him, and, tonight, I find myself wondering about his fiancée, my curiosity evolving into envy. Perhaps I could stay here, I'm thinking, start my own business and continue meeting Sione on the sly.

Later, when he falls asleep, I prop my head on my hand and look down at him. His long dark eyelashes rest on a wide cheek still plump with youth and with some sort of innocence, though certainly not inexperience.

When he wakes, he smiles his crooked smile and sits up. "You're not like your sister," he says.

I laugh. "That's the truth." Though Cheryl and I are only two years apart, we have never been anything alike. Always a sensitive kid, Cheryl nursed sick animals, wore her hair long and curly, and allowed so many stray cats on her bed that she barely had room to sleep. I possessed none of her dreaminess; I'd snipped my name from Melanie to Mel at the age of eight, wore my hair efficiently short, and was networking by the time I was in junior high. Cheryl had remained a virgin until college, until she fell in love; I'd done it at fourteen with a childhood friend to get it over with. And from there, we'd lived out our lives as one would expect: she became a social worker and eventually drifted out here, and I worked my way up the ladder of a global corporation. We've never shown much consideration for each other's work, and it amazes me even now, as I watch Sione pull on his clothes, that I've found something in Cheryl's environment to appreciate.

He dresses quickly. "What's your hurry?" I ask. He leans down, kisses my ear. "Car," he says. I don't hear anything, except the slap of the door as it closes behind him.

Yet a few minutes later, I hear the rumble of an engine, and then the door opens again. I grab Cheryl's robe, hoping Sione has come back.

But it's Cheryl in the living room. "Hi," she says. She leafs through the mail I picked up for her in town. "Was that Sione I just saw leaving?"

"Yes. You're back early."

"It went more smoothly than I thought," she says. "Was he here to see me?"

"Not exactly."

Then she notices I'm wearing her robe. "Did you let him in dressed like that?"

"No," I say, "I put it on after he left."

She puts her mail down. "What? Don't tell me you—"

"Well, you left me here with nothing to do," I say, "and I needed *something* to occupy my time. Sorry about your sheets—I'll wash them tomorrow."

"Are you crazy?" She puts her hands to her head, pulling them through her hair. She mutters something in Tongan, but her anger needs no translation.

"What's the big deal?" I say. "His fiancée will never know. We were very discreet."

"You can't just do this," she says. "Not here. Tongans have very strict social and moral codes. It's *'ulungāanga kovi*."

"It's what?"

"Completely unacceptable behavior," she says, sitting down, putting her hands over her eyes.

"When did you become such a prude?" I say. "Besides, I'm a *palangi*— I'm allowed to screw up."

She looks up at me. "This isn't New York, Mel. Things are different here. I'm very close to his family. His sister is my best friend."

"Don't worry," I say. "Nobody knows. We'll be discreet."

"No." She straightened abruptly. "Whatever's going on, you have to end it."

"I don't think that's your call to make."

"It is my call to make. It's over," she says, with a resolve I've never heard in her voice—flexible Cheryl, suddenly defiant. Instead of arguing until she sees it my way, I find myself raising my shoulders in a noncommittal shrug. Then I go to her room and strip the sheets from her bed.

Kalapu

When Cheryl invites me to the village kava party, she says it's a great honor for a *palangi* to be included. But I know the real reason: she wants to keep tabs on me. I agreed to stop seeing Sione, just to end the tension between us, but she didn't believe me. I've hardly been out of her sight since. *Here's your problem*, I told her: *you don't know how to be bad.* Her reply: *You don't know how to be good.*

At the party, the *kalapu*, we pour kava into cups for the men. As much as I'd like to toss back a few myself, the women, even *palangi*s, aren't allowed to drink kava, only to serve it.

I wear a floor-length skirt fitted with a *kiekie*, a long woven accessory that Cheryl wrapped around my waist for the occasion. We sit in the same circle as Sione, though he is careful not to look our way. As the men walk among the circles, talking and laughing, the women are silent, pouring kava and smiling pleasantly. I feel a headache throbbing at the back of my neck and wonder how soon we can leave.

We have to wait until the men have had enough. Cheryl stirs the kava with a reverence that is completely foreign to me. I have never seen the need to waste time on ceremony, on tradition. The *kalapu* stretches past midnight, and we leave around one in the morning, the men high and still drinking. Outside, we meet Siu—Cheryl's best friend, Sione's sister—near the family truck. Siu is shorter than either of us, and stocky, with flawless brown skin and a broad face framed by long black hair. She and Cheryl laugh and talk in a mix of Tongan and English.

"We're going home," Siu says. "You want a ride?"

"*'Io, mālō,*" Cheryl says. I join Cheryl and Siu in the cab, where their conversation slows. Cheryl has been quiet since I arrived, but it's hard to tell whether it's because of me or whether it's who she is now. When Siu stops in front of Cheryl's house, she says, "You're going to Blue Pacific now?"

Cheryl laughs. I noticed Blue Pacific when I was in town—a cheesy nightclub, the last place on earth you'd find Cheryl. "I'll see you tomorrow," Cheryl says, giving Siu a friendly thump on the arm.

"Remember, we cook next week."

"I remember," Cheryl says, jumping down to the dirt. "*'Alu ā.*"

"Cook for what?" I ask as we walk toward the house.

"Sione's wedding," Cheryl says. "I'm going to help them prepare for the feasts. There's one the day before the wedding, one the day of, and one the first Sunday after." Her voice sounds strangely tight. "You'll be gone by then."

"Why do you say that?" I reach the door first, stepping inside and pulling the string that turns on the overhead light while Cheryl pauses to take off her sandals.

"It's been two weeks," she says. "You have to get back to work, don't you?"

"I thought I'd extend my vacation. I'll help with the cooking."

Cheryl removes her *kiekie* and places it over one of the benches. "I think you should leave," she says quietly.

"You're kicking me out?" I'm hoping to provoke a retraction, an apology, but Cheryl says nothing.

I stand motionless in the shadows of her living room. "If you didn't want me here, you should have said something before I came from half-way around the world," I say. "I could've saved myself the airfare."

"You see?" she says. "It's always about you. And, for the record, I did want to see you—at first. I thought you were here to see me, too. But you're not. I don't even know why you're here."

I pause, cornered into an uneasy truth. "I lost my job," I say. "If you must know, I got fired."

"I'm sorry to hear that," Cheryl says.

I'm shocked by her nonchalance—by the fact that my sister, the great comforter, can find no empathy for me at all. "You know what my work means to me," I say. "It's my whole life."

"If it meant so much, Mel, why did you wait until now to tell me?" she says. "And why aren't you looking for another job? Are you so un-employable now that you plan on staying here forever?"

"No, that's you," I say, "not me." I immediately regret my words.

Cheryl sits and rubs her feet, then leans back in the chair. She looks at me for a long moment, and I can see, across the tanned skin of her face, cracks in the smooth foundation of her patience. She has always been so accepting, so tolerant of my capricious entries and exits into her life, and now she's giving up her long-standing role; she's redraw-ing the boundary lines of our relationship with a bold and unfamiliar flourish.

"I'm sorry," I say. "Let me stay. Please. Just another week."

Cheryl relents, or seems to. She retreats into her bedroom without another word.

Vava'u

When I first heard what had happened, I assumed someone else had screwed up—that was usually the way it worked. In this case, the error was so costly I knew immediately that jobs would be on the line. We were launching a new cellular handset, a high-speed smart phone that offered everything from music to photos to wireless Internet access. They called it e-Ba, and it would retail for $900, making it one of the most expensive handsets on the market. So, as much as clever advertising, we needed plenty of good publicity and word of mouth. My marketing plan included a sweepstakes—scratch-off cards to appear in the Sunday supplements of major newspapers, giving away a thousand e-Bas. It went brilliantly until the thousandth e-Ba was given away—and, to our horror, the winning scratch cards kept coming. First hundreds, then thousands. Then came the angry customers whose orders we couldn't fill, the news broadcasts calling it a "scam," the executive management team flying in from China. If we filled all the orders, we would be ruined. If we did not, the negative publicity would destroy us.

I vowed to get to the bottom of the disaster, to punish those responsible. We traced the mistake back to the print order, which read *ten* thousand instead of *one* thousand—an extra zero, typed in by someone's harried secretary. It was far too serious a typo for anyone to overlook. But at the bottom of the page, there it was: my signature, my approval. And when I saw the empty lines where my bosses' signatures should have been, the signatures I told myself that, despite the size and expense of the giveaway, weren't really necessary because I was competent enough to handle the job myself, I felt a seizing in my chest, a shortness of breath that I imagine people feel in the moment just before hearing bad news—the sudden, sickening knowledge that life as you've known it is about to change, possibly forever.

But the Kingdom of Tonga is not a place where global corporations launch new divisions; it's not a place where the *Wall Street Journal* is treated like the Bible. And it is not a place where you can pick up the latest issue of the *Harvard Business Review,* which now features a case study on the biggest marketing debacle in the history of the electronics industry. This is the reason I showed up on my sister's doorstep after so many years.

I'm now on Vava'u, at a youth hostel in Neiafu run by a German woman and her Tongan husband. For the sake of peace I offered to spend a week on one of Tonga's outer islands, and Cheryl seemed grateful. Our arrangement, while it resolved nothing else, made me feel as if I still possessed a modicum of negotiating power, despite having lost the argument over Sione. True to my word, I've stayed away from him. It's not easy, when I see him walking down the road in front of Cheryl's house or waving from his truck—he looks at me almost expressionless, mirroring my boredom. But I'm determined to be good, to prove Cheryl wrong, and I simply wave as he passes by.

The hostel's owners both speak English well, and apparently they've had a slow season because they sit with me on the covered porch all day long, bringing me bottles of Royal Tongan Beer and teaching me Tongan words and phrases.

The island seems to be home to a lot of expatriates. When I decide to go snorkeling, I charter a boat from an American woman. I'm glad that it's just the two of us, because Tongan women keep their arms and legs covered in public, and only in this relative privacy can I finally show my skin some sun. As I lounge on the boat's deck on our return to the island, the American tells me she came to Tonga on a round-the-world trip and never left.

"I fell in love," she says. "Me and Malakai have been together six years now."

"And you wanted to stay here," I ask, "instead of taking him to the States?"

"Oh, yeah," she says. "We've gone back a couple times, to visit, but life's better here."

"My sister is on Tongatapu," I say. "She did the same thing."

"Did she marry the guy?"

"No, there's no guy. She just stayed."

Cheryl makes little money because she doesn't need to; she and her friends take care of one another. She doesn't have rent, car payments, credit card bills. She doesn't wear makeup or new clothing and seems all the happier for it. She's always been like that—she never cared how much she made or what she wore—but she's finally found a place where that doesn't matter to anyone else either. Perhaps, in some way, my arrival has taken that from her, has reminded her that while she may live here, she's not truly home.

Fieme'atokoni

Siu's kitchen overflows with raw fish and meat, root vegetables and fruit—a scene that would give even a lax health inspector cause for alarm. Hands and arms and knives move with a frenzied choreography, and juices that shouldn't ever meet flow together. The smells are heavy, stifling.

Siu notices us standing in the doorway. "*Fieme'atokoni*," Cheryl tells her with a smile. "We're here to help you cook," she adds in English, for my benefit.

"Come in!" Siu cries. "We will put you to work."

Siu outlines the preparations: The men are gutting the pigs to roast over the spit. We women are to cut up the fruit, fillet the fish, and chop the potatoes and *'ufi* for the men to cook in the *'umu*, the underground oven. A couple of women are preparing *lu*, pele leaves filled with meat, coconut milk, tomato, and onion, which will be wrapped in tinfoil and baked. I'm just relieved that we don't have to handle the pigs.

After doing a supervisory lap around the kitchen, Siu brings me some more fruit, then picks up a knife and begins chopping. "You went to Vava'u on the weekend?" she asks in English. "Did you like it?"

" *'Io, aupito*," I answer, trying out some new Tongan words. Thinking of Vava'u's empty, sugary beaches and its walls of palms, I try to repeat a phrase the American had taught me. *"Na'e faka'ofo'ofa a e onioni,"* I say: *The sand was beautiful.*

Siu's hands freeze in mid-chop, suspended above a watermelon. She looks at Cheryl, then her face contorts. In confusion I turn to Cheryl, whose expression, long dormant, is one I recognize: barely suppressed laughter.

"What's so funny?" I ask, as they both burst out laughing. Though the joke is on me, at that moment I welcome it: I haven't seen my sister laugh since I arrived in Tonga.

"Where'd you learn that?" Cheryl asks as she catches her breath.

"She means *'one'one*," says Siu.

"I know," Cheryl says. She turns to me, leaning close with an intimacy we haven't shared since we were girls. "You just said that you think it's beautiful to be fucked up the ass."

I freeze as the enormity of my faux pas sinks in, remembering the others I'd shared that phrase with over the last few days—the village grocer, one of the kids in Cheryl's neighborhood. Was there anyone else?

"Don't worry," says Cheryl, smiling. "You're a *palangi*." She looks at Siu with such warmth and affection that I feel as if I've vanished from the kitchen. They begin talking again, in English, to include me, but I stay quiet. No matter what language they speak, the nature of their bond is indecipherable to me.

Mali

The night before Sione's wedding, I join Cheryl and Siu serving kava at a formal ceremony for the bride's and the groom's families and other prominent members of the village. It goes late, and I feel as though I can barely stand by the time we go out to Siu's truck. Cheryl says she forgot her backpack and goes back inside, and I lean against the door of the truck.

"Our *mali* tomorrow," Siu says, "will be your first Tongan wedding."

"And my last," I say.

"Leaving so soon?"

"I think so." I haven't reserved my flight home, but I can tell that Cheryl is anxious for me to do so. I twist around and press my forehead against the passenger-side window. I see Cheryl's backpack on the floor.

"I'll be right back," I tell Siu, and head back to find Cheryl. She is not easy to find, and I poke my head in door after door. I turn a corner and see shadows at the end of the hall. When I realize what I've just seen, I step back, flattening my body against the wall, thinking that I must be high off kava fumes. But another look confirms it—Cheryl and Sione, wrapped in each other's arms, lips, eyes. I force myself to back away, slowly.

Siu and I wait by the car for another ten minutes or so, then Cheryl runs out. "I can't find my pack anywhere," she says breathlessly.

"It's in the truck," I tell her.

"Oh," she says. "Sorry I kept you waiting."

I don't say anything, and neither does Cheryl. When we get home, she says she's tired, and she goes right to bed. I can't sleep and finally get up and step outside. Out in the yard, I pace around, something I used to do at the office when I had action items to address. I don't know how to handle what I've discovered. Suddenly, I'm a marketer again, with newfound competitive intelligence, thinking of strategy and spin.

I hear an abrupt snort. I turn, and just a few feet away I see the gleaming eyes of the red pig, menacing in the dark. I stop moving and stand still, trying to remember whether it has teeth, and, if so, how big they are. The pig watches me with beady, glittering eyes. We stare at each other, each trying to assess whether the other aims to do harm.

After what feels like an hour, the pig decides I'm safe and lowers its head back to the ground, snuffling in the dirt. I back slowly away, keeping my eyes on it until I'm inside the house. I return to bed, listening to the pig's nocturnal scavenging, and decide, for once, that immediate reactions, to anything, are not always the best kind.

Sione marries Lotu in a formal ceremony. Cheryl and I join them afterward for the *kaipola*, the feast, and then we help them with another tradition, moving the bride's bedroom to her new house.

I watch my sister closely as we load Lotu's bedroom furniture onto the wide flat bed of a cousin's truck. We lift the mattress together, and her face across its broad expanse looks calmer than I expect.

We unload the furniture in Sione and Lotu's new house and rearrange it in the connubial bedroom, exactly as it had appeared in Lotu's old room. When we're finished, Cheryl lingers in the room for a moment after everyone leaves. Tonight, she has told me, Sione and Lotu will spend the night here, but they won't consummate their marriage until Sunday.

Later, when I emerge from a shower, I'm not surprised to see that Cheryl has helped herself to the whiskey I'd bought for myself and Sione. I fill a large cup and top hers off before sitting down.

"I saw you and Sione," I say, "at the kava party."

She takes a drink. "We've been together for three years," she says. "Longer than he's been engaged to Lotu."

"Why didn't you tell me?"

"The same way you tell me everything?" she says. "Besides, what difference would it make?"

"Well, I wouldn't have slept with him, for one thing," I say.

Cheryl raises her eyebrows.

"Oh, come on," I say. "He's the one you should be pissed at. He wasn't exactly hard to seduce."

"I know who he is, Mel," she says.

I let a mouthful of whiskey slide down my throat, stinging on its way. "What happens now?"

"He gets married. I get over it. That's it."

"Does anyone know?"

She shakes her head. "Like I said, the family is too traditional. I knew from the beginning nothing would ever come of it."

"Well," I say, "I guess we have something in common after all."

She finishes her whiskey in one long drink and sets her cup on the floor. "I guess we do."

Sai pe

On *'uluaki Sapate*, First Sunday, Cheryl and I join the families for the feast. Later, we wait outside Sione and Lotu's house with the women of the family. Cheryl chats with Siu and Lotu's relatives, but I'm less at ease. Inside, Sione and Lotu are consummating their marriage, and the family is waiting outside to be presented with a bloodied sheet.

I look at the door of the house, listening only vaguely to the conversation around me, the full, rounded words that I can't understand. I wonder whether Lotu and her family believe that Sione is a virgin, or whether they care.

I hear someone say, *"Fēfē hake?"* and Cheryl answers: *"Sai pe"*—*I'm well*. I glance over at her and see that she has one eye practically glued to the door herself, and I know that she isn't.

Shortly Sione emerges from the house, dressed and carrying a white sheet. He stands before Lotu's aunt and offers it with both hands. I see smears of pinkish blood. He says something in Tongan.

Cheryl and I head back to her house. She walks as if she were hollow inside. "I can stay a while longer," I say. "For you, this time, not for me. If you want."

"That's okay," she says. "I'll be fine."

"I don't mind. It's the least I can do."

"No, really," she says. "I do better alone."

In this way, too, we are alike.

In the house, I pick up the phone to reserve my flight. But it's dead; like most services in Tonga, phones work only sporadically. "Guess I'm here for another day or so anyway," I say.

"What are you going to do when you go back?"

I shrug. "Maybe I'll write a book. It worked for Jayson Blair. I'll call it 'You May Already Be a Winner.'"

She smiles. "Well," she says, "you always do land on your feet."

"What about you?" I ask.

"Oh, I'll stay here," she says.

Even without Sione? I want to ask, but when I open my mouth, I say instead, "What did Sione say afterward, to Lotu's aunt?"

"He said, 'You've raised your daughter well.'"

We go to bed early, and I awaken later, needing to visit the outhouse. As I pass by the window, I hear a faint noise outside, like voices. Straining to see, I eventually make out two shapes, heads together, walking slowly toward a corner of the yard. I recognize Cheryl and Sione, but then they fold themselves into a blanket, their bodies one, and disappear into the shadows. I turn away from the window. When I return to my makeshift bed, I lie awake for a long time. From my place inside the house, with Cheryl and Sione hidden somewhere among the trees outside, I sense that my sister and I are finally aligned, in a constellation we can accept if not comprehend, just beyond one another's vision, yet just within reach. I listen for the sounds of them, but I hear only the tolerant red pig muttering in the yard and the camouflaging palms whispering in the dark.

TRANSLATION MEMORY

In the airport terminal, Dan Marxen's wife slips a pill between her lips as he pretends not to notice. The little white pills look as innocuous as aspirin, but for Julie they have become as necessary as water—and because she lets them dissolve under her tongue instead of swallowing them, by the time they board she will already be in a dreamy, hypnagogic state.

After takeoff, she lets her head fall toward his. "Did you know," she asks sleepily, "that Japan has an earthquake every five minutes?"

He looks up from his laptop. "No," he says, "I didn't."

Her eyes flutter at half mast, then close. He thinks of the bottle of Maker's Mark in the overhead, his gift for Keiji and the other executives at Saito Electronics, and wishes he could down a finger or two before the flight attendants start making their rounds.

The twelve-hour flight seems to last far longer, and by the time they reach Tokyo Dan feels as dazed as Julie looks. They stumble through baggage claim and customs to find the driver Saito has sent for them, a thin, round-faced man named Yamaguchi. The drive downtown will take more than an hour. Julie swallows another Ativan and drifts back to sleep as Dan watches the oncoming lights rush at them on the highway. At the hotel, he takes off her shoes and eases her into bed, folding her arms across her chest and tucking the blankets up around her chin. He looks at her for a moment, then moves her arms down to her sides.

Then he returns to the streets. Shinjuku is alive with neon light, with the ringing of *pachinko* machines bursting out from behind automatic sliding glass doors. A few streets north, women approach him from the doorways of clubs, inviting him for drink, for dancing, for massage.

He passes a McDonald's. Inside, a group of *gaijin*, Americans most likely, are eating Big Macs and drinking coffee. He thinks of the presentation on Web globalization he will give tomorrow. *Use a splash global gateway to direct first-time visitors to local content*, he will tell Saito's executives. *Keep a global link in the upper right corner of each page so that users will always be able to find their way back to the local home page.* The advice, he realizes, is universal; no matter what the context, people want to feel close to home.

He is not tired but returns to the room, where Julie is sleeping soundly, almost too soundly. Dan turns on the television, volume low, and finds a local news station. He listens to the comforting sounds of the unfamiliar language, absolving him of thought, until he sees an ad in English for Mt. Rainier coffee, its packaging a blatant Starbucks knockoff. He makes a few notes and looks over at Julie again. She hasn't moved. He leans down close, feels her light breath on his cheek.

On the morning Julie got laid off, he had been in the hallway at his office in Cambridge, looking out a window, watching a hawk dismantle its prey. It was a sunless June day, and a storm was brewing, the clouds growing portentously dark. Dan had gotten up to stretch his legs after a ninety-minute conference call when a movement across the street caught his eye. He went to the window and stood mesmerized, even as he heard the distant, urgent ring of his cell phone. Atop a telephone pole, the hawk was methodically plucking feathers from a captured pigeon. Fluff and quill drifted down onto the street. Though he didn't know it at the time, as the pigeon shrank to flesh, Julie was across the river packing her desk.

Later he walked through the feathers in the parking lot and drove home to find her standing by a window facing the street, in a posture not unlike his own that morning. He stood behind her for a while, trying to see what it was she was looking at until he realized it was nothing.

The layoff wasn't the true loss, for either of them. That loss had occurred three months earlier, and, ironically, it had been for the sake of her job. *We've still got plenty of time,* Julie said then, adding, with uncanny accuracy, *After all, I won't have this position forever.*

She still referred to it as *the procedure.*

For days afterward he had come home to find her in the same spot she occupied now, staring at the empty street. When she turned to him, her eyes looked like thin wet glass, as if the slightest sound could shatter them. And so he said nothing, until she asked if she could accompany him to Japan.

Again he stands at the window, this time viewing the pink summit of Mount Fuji beyond the maze of Tokyo's skyscrapers. He turns away and takes his watch and wallet out of the hotel desk and then picks up his laptop. He glances over at Julie. She's rolled onto her side, her hand under her chin, looking, to his relief, more asleep now than unconscious.

Keiji meets him at the entrance to the Saito building and ushers him past security. They walk through halls of polished linoleum and stark white walls, reminding Dan of the hospital where he took Julie. She'd suffered complications after the abortion, blood loss and scarring that the doctor said would not hinder her fertility, but Julie was not yet convinced.

He suddenly feels too warm and loosens his tie. He notices that all of the men and women in the building are in shirtsleeves, and he slips off his jacket.

He discovers later that Japanese companies are participating in a national energy-saving program that requires them to keep their building temperatures in the low eighties during the summer months. He tries to be subtle as he wipes sweat off his brow, his upper lip. He hopes no one notices the wet spots on his shirt.

But even as the sweat trickles down his back, he has to admire the culture of economy—in Japan, everything is scarce: resources, space, time. Through working with Saito and his other accounts, he has come to appreciate Japanese efficiency. He wonders, as he tastes salt on his lips, whether the withdrawal of affection between himself and Julie is perhaps not likewise a matter of economizing—not a falling away of love but a storage of energy for the future. He hopes that what they are doing is not holding out but holding in reserve.

He tells the executives that nothing can replace what globalization experts call *depth of content.* "You can't globalize your Web site halfway," he explains. "It's better to do it all at once, or not at all. You'll run into problems if you offer only one or two pages in your target language. What happens when a Brazilian user lands on his local site, clicks through, and ends up back at a Japanese page?"

He watches Keiji and his colleagues nod in agreement. "You are say-ing we need more than a façade?" Keiji asks.

"Exactly," Dan says. He catches a drop of sweat at his eyebrow.

That night, his eyes begin to blur from hours of staring at his laptop. He shuts the lid and picks up the Tokyo guidebook that Julie bought before the trip. She doesn't seem to mind; she's watching Larry King on CNN International, her eyes gazing at the screen almost unblinking. He opens the book to a page with a folded-down corner and scans it to see what she might have earmarked. He finds an entry for the Buddhist temple Zozo-ji. *Jizo, the deity that looks after aborted or miscarried fetuses . . . The temple grounds are filled with tiny statues given by parents as offerings to Jizo . . . A place of worship and remembrance . . .*

His chest tightens, and he sits up to take a breath. Julie, hazy on Ativan, doesn't notice. Has she been to Zozo-ji already? He looks at her, her face unanimated, dull. She is still beautiful, her skin pale and smooth from years of avoiding the sun, her cinnamon hair streaked with a few strands of gray. He has always loved the gray, as much as she complains about it. Whenever he sees the silver catching the light, he glimpses their future.

She leans back into a pillow and closes her eyes. He places the book back on the nightstand, leaving the corner of the page folded down.

"When used effectively," he tells the Saito group, "translation memory can shave 30 to 50 percent off your translation costs."

He explains how it works, using a PowerPoint slide showing two pages of text placed side by side. "The TM software," he says, "highlights previously translated source material, and this saves you the cost of retranslating the same content. It's not a perfect science, though. You'll have exact matches some of the time; sometimes you'll have what's called a 'fuzzy match.' You'll still need an editor to verify the content, but because translators charge by the word, the savings with TM can be tremendous."

But it takes a while, he adds, to build translation memory.

This is what he remembers: the day he and Julie met, five years ago, at an outdoor jazz festival on Boston Common, ten minutes before a thunderstorm sent them into the lobby of a boutique hotel.

He remembers martinis in a dim lounge, emerging later to a clearing summer sky.

No, it wasn't the Federalist, she had said at a recent dinner party, when someone asked how they met. *It was Number Nine Park.*

Then he remembers being told about the pregnancy, arguing that though it was unplanned, they would make it work, refusing to drive her to the clinic but having no choice later, when the bleeding wouldn't stop.

He remembers her saying, weeks afterward, *We agreed on this,* and being unable to convince her that they did not.

This is what happens when they lay out their memories side by side. At best, they are a fuzzy match.

That afternoon, an earthquake strikes Chiba state, in the east, as Dan stands with his laser pointer at the front of Saito's main conference room. He won't find out until later that its magnitude was 5.8 and that there was moderate damage at the epicenter. One minute he's suggesting designs for a global template, and the next he's swaying on his feet, wondering if it's the jet lag, or if the heat of the room is making him dizzy. No one says anything. *An earthquake every five minutes,* he reminds himself, and keeps talking.

That evening, Julie skips her dose of Ativan and joins him for his dinner with the Saito execs at an upscale Japanese restaurant. He watches her feign interest in something Keiji is saying. The topic changes to sightseeing, and he hears her ask about Zozo-ji. He holds his breath.

"It was the temple of the Tokugawa family—the famous shogun," says Keiji.

Aiko, the only woman executive, adds, "It is also known for the Jizo statues."

"I read about that," Julie says. She doesn't look his way.

"So you know that people go to Zozo-ji to do *mizuko kuyo,*" Aiko continues.

He watches Julie shake her head.

"It is a ritual," Aiko says. *"Mizuko* means 'water baby.' People do *mizuko kuyo* to give the spirit good wishes for its next life."

"Some do it because of *tatari,*" Keiji adds.

"What do you mean?" Julie's brow furrows.

"Sometimes the *mizuko* are angry," Keiji says, "and parents do the rituals so the spirits will not take revenge."

"It is a nice practice," Aiko says, overriding him. She begins to explain the ritual to Julie, and at the same time Keiji begins telling Dan about the sumo matches in Ryogoku, and Dan tries to listen to both of them, his ear tuning more into Aiko. Yet he hears only fragments: monthly ceremonies, priests, drums, chanting.

The conversations ebb and swirl onto other topics. Dan watches Julie for signs of anxiety or grief; without the Ativan, he doesn't know what to expect. Yet she looks calmer and more composed than she has since they arrived—than in weeks, as a matter of fact. She eats her noodles delicately as those around her slurp with unself-conscious gusto.

It feels as if they've been sitting at the long, low table forever; Dan's knees ache, his legs bent awkwardly on the floor. He looks around the table, at the cornucopia before them: bowls of rice and soup, long plates of tofu and sushi, round dishes of pickled vegetables and dried fish, seashells filled with mussels simmering over open flames, sake and sweet wine. He recalls reading that the Japanese have a word for a fifth taste, *umami,* used to describe an otherwise indescribable flavor: something savory, something good. He tries to conjure *umami* as he sips a thick *miso,* but his tongue registers only bitterness.

Back in the hotel room, the pile of loose change that he'd left on the desk is stacked neatly next to the phone. A bag of Japanese rice snacks he'd taken from the mini bar and left open on the bed has been sealed and placed on the bedside table.

Julie drops her purse on the desk and perches on the bed nearest the door, the one she claimed as hers the night they arrived. She looks at him, her cheeks warm with color, her eyes bright. *It's the sake,* he thinks.

"So," she asks, "did you hear what they said about Zozo-ji?"

"Of course," he said.

"Well, what do you think?"

Sometimes the mizuko are angry. "I'm not sure."

"Maybe we should go see it."

"Are you worried about what Keiji said? That we need to pacify an angry spirit?"

"No, it's not that. Don't make fun."

"I'm not," he said. "I'm serious."

"So do you want to go?"

"I don't know. Do you?"

"I guess it could give us a chance to start over," she says. "Offer an apology to the *mizuko.* Ask for forgiveness."

He thinks, *Who are you asking?*

"Tomorrow's our last day," she says.

It's not yet noon, but the air is feverishly hot, the city draped in a gauzy haze. Dan feels the moisture cling to his skin, as if his body is clenched in a sweaty fist. He and Julie walk along a wide boulevard toward Zozo-ji, then through the vast grounds of the temple. In front of the main hall, Dan watches a young couple toss a few coins into a collection box and pull the rope that rings the bell. They stand praying for several minutes and then clap three times before turning away.

Julie has wandered away from him, and when he looks to the right, he sees her approaching a courtyard filled with hundreds of tiny statues, lined up row after row toward the back of the main hall: the water babies.

The statues stand about two feet tall, and they have been dressed in little red knit caps and sweaters. Some wear bibs; others wear T-shirts gaping with empty sleeves. The clothes are tattered, moldy from rainfall and faded by the sun. Beside them, plastic pinwheels whir in the intermittent breeze, alongside containers of flowers and candy, or toys. As he turns down another row, Dan sees Japanese characters written in white on the backs of the statues, and he wishes he could read them.

Three schoolchildren speed by on bicycles, laughing and shouting, on a sidewalk adjacent to the temple. He and Julie are walking down different paths now, looking at the faces of the statues. Dan finally finds one that looks peaceful, its tiny hands folded in a prayer, its red knit cap and bib dirty and damp, its face serene. Next to it is a batch of dead daisies in a plastic vase. He stands looking at it until he feels Julie beside him.

"Aiko said you can buy the statues and bring them here," she says. "Maybe we should've bought one."

"I didn't think about that."

"I didn't know where to get them. But I did bring this." She holds up a pink wind-up Gloomy Bear, a ubiquitous Japanese toy.

"Do you like this one?" she asks, indicating the statue that caught his eye. He nods, and she places the toy in front of the statue, under its praying hands.

Back in Cambridge, two weeks after returning from Japan, he feels sluggish and dazed, as if he's still fighting jet lag. He pushes his chair away from his desk and stands, stretching. He walks into the hall, pausing near the window where he watched the hawk that day, months ago. The telephone pole is bare.

He returns to his office, to the long list of emails and the blinking message light on his phone. Two new mergers in the past week have made waves in the industry—two translation agencies and two software providers—everything, it seems, is merging, advancing. He is still working with Saito on its nascent Web globalization project. They are balking at the costs: they want to see definitive returns; they want proof that their investment will pay off. *It's a worthwhile gamble*, he tells them, but he can't back it up with anything but his own faith.

He understands their impatience.

Sometimes, late at night when he is wide awake and it is morning in Japan, he can close his eyes and see them: the rows of Jizo statues, upright as headstones. He can see Julie's hair that day, the wind separating the long, wavy strands and revealing the gray.

And he can still see the face of the small figure to which they bequeathed the toy. He'd stayed a few moments after Julie left, regarding the water baby before him. He had reached out his hand, as if he might bridge the liminal divide between their two worlds. He'd touched its cap, the fabric warm and moist in the humid air, then moved his hand to its face. It was gritty and stone cold.

THE ECSTATIC CRY

One of our gentoo chicks is missing.

I flip through our field notebook to find Thom's chart of the colony, then match nest to nest. According to our records, the chick was two weeks old, but now the rocky nest is empty, the adult penguins gone. I search but find no remains; its disappearance must have been the work of a predatory skua. When skuas swoop down to snatch chicks or eggs, they leave little behind.

I move away from the colony and sit on a rock to make some notes. That's when I hear it—a distinctly human yelp, and a thick noise that I have heard only once in my life and have never forgotten: the sound of bone hitting something solid.

I jump up and see a man lying in the snow, a red-jacketed tourist from the *M/S Royal Albatross*, which dropped its anchor in our bay this morning. He'd fallen hard, landing on his back and apparently narrowly missing a gentoo, which is still scurrying away. The man doesn't move.

I hold still for a moment, hoping he will get up. Then I start toward him.

Fifteen other tourists are within thirty yards, yet no one else seems to notice. They're still up the hill, listening to their ship's naturalist, the whirs and blips of their digital cameras obscuring all other sounds on the island.

But my research partner, Thom, must have seen something; he gets to the man first. And now a woman is scrambling guardedly down the same hill, taking care, despite her hurry, to avoid the same fate.

I turn my attention to the man. The blood staining the snow beneath his head is an unwelcome sight, bright and thin amid the ubiquitous dark pink guano of the penguins and replete with new bacteria, which could be deadly for the birds. I stifle an urge to start cleaning it up.

Thom's voice snatches back my attention. "Deb," he says sharply, glancing up. He spent two years in medical school before turning to marine biology, and he looks uncharacteristically nervous. By now, four more tourists in their matching red jackets have gathered around us, and it's obvious that Thom wants to shield them from what he sees.

I hold out my arms and move forward, forcing the red jackets back a couple of steps. The woman who'd hurried down the hill is trying to look past me. She seems younger than the usual middle-aged passengers who cruise down to Antarctica, the ones who have already been every-where else, who want to check off their seventh continent. "Are you with him?" I ask her. "Where's your guide?"

"No—I don't know," she stutters. Blond hair trails from under her hat into her eyes, wide with an anxiety I can't place. "He's up there, maybe." She motions toward the gentoo colony. I glance up. The hill has nearly disappeared in fog.

"Someone needs to find him," I say. "And we need the doctor from the boat. Who's he traveling with?"

"His wife, I think," someone answers.

"Get her."

I kneel next to Thom, who's examining the man's head. Were we anywhere but Antarctica, the injury might not seem as critical. But we are at the bottom of the world, days from the nearest city, even farther from the nearest trauma center. There is, of course, a doctor along on the cruise, and basic medical facilities at Palmer Station, half an hour away by boat—but it's unclear whether that will be enough.

The man hasn't moved since he fell. A deep gash on the back of his head has bled through the thick wad of gauze that Thom has applied. Voices approach—the guide, the wife, the doctor. The man's chest sud-denly begins heaving, and Thom quickly reaches out and turns his head so he will vomit into the snow. More bacteria.

The man shudders and makes a feeble effort to sit up, then loses con-sciousness again. Thom presses fresh gauze to his head.

"What happened?" the wife cries.

"He slipped," I tell her.

Thom and I move aside for the doctor.

"How could this happen?" the wife wails. It's no mystery, I want to tell her; her husband is about sixty pounds overweight and can't see his own feet, which are stuffed into cheap boots despite the fact that he probably paid ten thousand dollars for the tour that brought him here. But I silently place a hand on her shoulder as crew members show up with a gurney. "We need to get him to Palmer," the doctor says, her voice low. The man remains still.

Thom helps them load him onto the gurney, and they carry him to a Zodiac. I get a plastic bag from our camp, then return to the scene and begin scooping up the bloody, vomit-covered snow. We're in one of the last pristine environments in the world, and we go to great lengths to protect the animals from anything foreign. Visitors sterilize their boots before setting foot on the island, and again when they depart. No one leaves without everything they came with. Yet sometimes, like now, it seems pointless. Injuries like this are unusual, but I've seen tourists drop used tissues and gum wrappers, not knowing or not caring enough to pick them up. I want to chase after them, to show them our data, to tell them how much the fate of penguins has changed as more and more tourists pass through these islands. But Thom and I must be patient with this red-jacketed species—we are employed by the same tour company that brings them here. The company sponsors our research, and in turn it gets a tax break and two more experts to give onboard lectures and slide shows. With government dollars harder and harder to come by, I'm grateful—but we earn it more each season, and our work often has to take a backseat to keeping the tourists happy.

Thom returns and stands over me, watching for a moment. Then he says, "They need me to go to Palmer with them."

I look up. "Why?"

"The crew is crazed," he says, "and they need someone to stay with the victim and his wife."

"I guess we're at their mercy." I inspect the ground to make sure there's nothing left in the snow. Thom doesn't have a choice—we're often asked to fill in for the crew—but I know what he is really asking me. We have been partners for three years, and I've never spent a night on this island alone.

I stand up. Thom is short, and I'm tall, so we look each other directly in the eye. "Go ahead. I'll be all right."

"You sure?"

"I'll keep the radio on, just in case. But yeah, I'll be fine. After all this, I'll enjoy the peace."

"I'll be back tomorrow," he says.

We return to camp, a trio of tents not far from the bay. From there we can watch the ships approach and, more important, depart.

Another Zodiac is waiting to take Thom to Palmer. He collects a few things from his tent and gives my shoulder a squeeze before he leaves. "I'll buzz you later," he says. He smiles, and I feel a sudden, sharp loneliness, like an intake of cold air.

I watch the Zodiac disappear around the outer cliffs of the bay, then turn back to our empty camp.

It's hard to believe on an evening like this, with the air sogged with rain and the penguins splashing in a pool of slush nearby, that Antarctica is the biggest desert in the world, the driest place on earth. The Dry Valleys have not seen rain for millions of years, and thanks to the cold, nothing rots or decays. Even up here, on the peninsula, I've seen hundred-year-old seal carcasses in perfect condition and abandoned whaling stations frozen in time. Those that perish in Antarctica—penguins, seals, explorers—are immortalized, the ice preserving life in the moment of death.

But for all that stays the same here, Antarctica is constantly changing. Every year, the continent doubles in size as the ocean freezes around it; the ice shelf shifts; glaciers calve off. Whales once hunted are now protected; krill once ignored are now trawled; land once desolate now sees thousands of tourists a season. But it remains, to me, a place of illusion. When I'm here, I still feel comfortably isolated, even though increasingly I am not.

I make myself a cold, unappetizing supper of leftover pasta and think of my return, two weeks away. Thom and I will be eating well then, cozily aboard the *Royal Albatross*, with its gourmet meals and full bar. And my sense of aloneness will be gone, replaced with lectures and slide shows and endless Q&A sessions.

I finish my supper and clean up, careful not to leave even the smallest crumbs behind. At nearly ten o'clock, it's still bright outside, the sun still hours away from its brief disappearance. I take a walk, heading up toward the colony that was so heavily trafficked today, the one the man visited before he fell. The empty nest remains deserted. The other penguins are still active, bringing rocks back to fortify their nests, feeding their chicks. Some are sitting on eggs; others are returning from the sea to reunite with their mates, greeting one another with their call of recognition, a high-pitched rattling squawk.

I sit down on a rock, about fifteen feet from the nearest nest, and watch the birds amble up the trail from the water. They appear to ignore me, but I know this isn't true—I know that their heart rates increase when I walk past, that they move faster when I'm around. Thom and I are studying the two largest penguin colonies here, tracking their numbers and rate of reproduction, to gauge the effects of tourism and human contact. Our island is one of the most frequently visited spots in Antarctica, and our data shows that the birds have noticed. They're experiencing symptoms of stress: lower birth rates, fewer fledging chicks. It's a strange irony that the hands that feed our research are the same hands that guide the boats here every season, and I sometimes wonder what will happen when the results of our five-year study are published.

Often, when I watch the penguins, I forget I'm a scientist. I become so mesmerized by their purrs and squawks, by the precision of their clumsy waddle, that I forget I have another life, somewhere else—that I have an apartment in Eugene, that I teach marine biology at the University of Oregon, that I'm forty-two years old and not yet on a tenure track, that I haven't had a real date in three years. I forget that my life now is only as good as my next grant and that, when the money dries up, I'm afraid that I will, too.

I first came to Antarctica when I was thirty, to study the emperor penguins at McMurdo. I've been returning every season I can, to whatever site I can, by whatever means. Thom and I have two seasons left in our study. He's married, with two small kids at home; this will be it for him. I'm still looking for another way to make it back.

What I'd like most is to return to the Ross Sea, to the emperor penguins. This is the species that captivates me—the only Antarctic bird that breeds in winter, right on the ice. Emperors don't build nests; they live entirely on fast ice and in the water, never setting foot on solid land. I love that during breeding season, the female lays her egg, then scoots it over to the male and takes off, traveling a hundred miles across the frozen ocean to open water and swimming away to forage for food.

She comes back when she's fat and ready to feed her chick.

My mother, still hopeful about marriage and grandkids for her only daughter, says that this is my problem, that I think like an emperor. I expect a man to sit tight and wait patiently while I disappear across the ice. I don't build nests.

When the female emperor returns, she uses a signature call to find her partner. Reunited, the two move in close and bob their heads toward each other, shoulder to shoulder in an armless hug, raising their beaks in what we call the ecstatic cry. Penguins are romantics. Most mate for life.

In the summer, sunsets last forever. They surrender not to darkness but to an overnight dusk, a grayish light that dims around midnight. As I prepare to turn in, I hear the splatter of penguins bathing in their slush, the barely perceptible pat of their webbed feet on the rocks.

Inside my tent, I extinguish my lamp and set a flashlight nearby, turning over a few times to find a comfortable angle. The rocks are ice-cold, the padding under my sleeping bag far too thin. As I finally put my head down, I hear a loud splash, clearly made by something much larger than a penguin—yet the ship is long gone. And when you're alone in Antarctica, you are truly alone.

Feeling suddenly uneasy, I turn my lamp on again. I grab my flashlight and a jacket and hurry outside, toward the rocky beach.

I can see a shape in the water, but it's bulky and oddly shaped, not smooth and sleek, like a seal. I shine my flashlight on it and see only red.

A man, in his cruise-issued parka, in the water up to his waist, looks into the glare of my flashlight. I stand there, too stunned to move.

Then the man turns away and steps further into the water. *He's crazy*, I think. *Why would he go in deeper?* Sometimes the seasick medication that tourists take causes odd and even troubling behavior, but I've never witnessed anything like this. As I watch him anxiously from the shore, I think of Ernest Shackleton. I think of the choices he made at every step to save the lives of his crew—his decision to abandon the *Endurance* in the Weddell Sea, to separate his crew and set out across the frozen water in search of land, to take a 22-foot rescue boat across eight hundred miles of open sea. I also think of Robert Scott, leading his team to their deaths just as his competitor became the first to reach the South Pole— and of the expedition guides who last year drove a Zodiac underneath the arc of a floating iceberg, only to have the berg calve and flip their boat, drowning the driver. In Antarctica, every decision is weighty, every outcome either a tragedy or a miracle.

Now, it seems, my own moment has come. It would be unthinkable to stand here and watch this man drown, but attempting a rescue could be even more dangerous. I'm alone. I'm wearing socks and a light jacket. The water is freezing or a few degrees above, and though I'm five-nine and strong, this man is big enough to pull me under if he wanted to, or if he panicked.

Perhaps Shackleton only believed he had options. Here, genuine options are few.

As I enter the icy water, my feet numb within seconds. The man is now in up to his chest, and by the time I reach him, he's thoroughly disoriented. He doesn't resist when I clutch his arms, pulling them over my shoulders and turning us toward shore. In the water he is almost a dead weight, but I feel a slight momentum behind me as I drag him toward the beach. Our progress is slow. Once on land, he's near collapse, and it takes all my strength to heave him up the rocks and into Thom's tent.

He crumples on the tent floor, and I strip off his parka, boots, and socks. Water spills over Thom's sleeping bag and onto his books. "Take off your clothes," I say, turning to rummage through Thom's things. I toss him a pair of sweatpants, the only thing of Thom's that will stretch to fit his tall frame, and two pairs of thick socks. I continue my search and find a couple of large T-shirts and an oversized sweater. When I turn back to him, the man has put on the sweats and is feebly attempting the socks, his hands shaking so badly that he can hardly command them. Impatiently, I reach over to help, yanking the socks onto his feet.

"What the hell were you thinking?" I demand, not really expecting an answer. I hardly look at him as I take off his shirt and help him squeeze into Thom's sweater. I turn on a battery-powered blanket and unzip Thom's sleeping bag. "Get in," I say. "You need to warm up."

His whole body shudders. He climbs in and pulls the blanket up to cover his shoulders.

"What are you doing here?" I ask. I, too, am shaking from the cold. "What the hell happened?"

He lifts his eyes, briefly. "The boat—it left me behind."

"That's impossible." I stare at him, but he won't look at me. "The *Royal Albatross* always does head counts. They count twice. No one's ever been left behind."

He shrugs. "Until now."

I think about the chaos of earlier that day. It's conceivable that this stranger could have slipped through the cracks.

"I'm calling Palmer. Someone will have to come out to take you back." I rise to my knees, eager to go first to my tent for dry clothes, then to the supply tent, where we keep the radio.

I feel his hand on my arm. "Do you have to do that just yet?" He smiles, awkwardly, his teeth knocking together. "It's just that—I've been here so long already, and I'm not ready to face the ship. It's embarrassing, to be honest with you."

"Don't you have someone who knows you're missing?" I regard him for the first time as a man, rather than an alien in my world. His face is pale and clammy, its lines suggesting he is my age or older, perhaps in his late forties. I glance down to look for a wedding band, but his fingers are bare. Following my gaze, he tucks his hands under the blanket. Then he shakes his head. "I'm traveling alone."

"Have you taken any medication? For seasickness?"

"No," he says. "I was in the Navy. I don't get seasick."

"Well," I say, "your boat's probably miles away by now, and we need to get you on it before it goes any farther."

He looks at me directly for the first time. "Don't," he says.

I'm still kneeling on the floor of the tent. "What do you think?" I ask. "That you can just stay here? That no one will figure out you're missing?"

He doesn't answer. "Look," I tell him, "it was an accident. No one's going to blame you for getting left behind."

"It wasn't an accident," he says. "I saw that other guy fall. I watched everything. I figured that if I stayed they probably wouldn't notice me missing."

I stand up. "I'll be right back."

He reaches up and grasps my wrist, so fast I don't have time to pull away. I'm surprised by how quickly his strength has come back.

I ease back down to my knees, and he loosens his grip. He looks at me through tired, heavy eyes—a silent plea. He's not scary, I realize then, but scared.

"In another month," I tell him, as gently as I can manage, "the ocean will freeze solid, and so will everything else, including you."

"What about you?"

"In a couple weeks, I'm leaving, too. Everyone leaves."

"Even the penguins?" The question, spoken through still-chattering teeth, lends him an innocence that almost makes me forgive his intrusions.

"Yes," I say. "Even they go north."

He doesn't respond, and I stand up again. He lets me leave, and I go straight to the radio in our supply tent, hardly thinking about my wet clothes. Just as I'm contacting Palmer, I realize that I don't know his name. I go back and poke my head inside. "Dennis Singleton," he says.

The dispatcher at Palmer tells me that they'll pick up Dennis in the morning, when they bring Thom back. "Unless it's an emergency," he says. "Everything okay?"

I want to tell him it's not okay, that this man might be crazy, dangerous, sick. But I can't exaggerate without risking never being taken seriously again—too big a risk with two more seasons of research here. So I say, "We're fine. Tell Thom we'll see him in the morning."

I return to the tent. Dennis has not moved. He is staring at a spot in the corner, and he barely acknowledges me.

His quietness is unsettling. "What were you doing in the water?" I ask.

"Thought I'd try to catch up to the boat," he says.

"Very funny. I'm serious."

He doesn't reply. A moment later, he asks, "What are *you* doing here?"

"Research, obviously."

"I know," he says. "But why come here, to the end of the earth?"

"What kind of question is that?"

"You know what I mean," he says. "You have to be a real loner, to enjoy being down here." He rubs the fingers of his left hand. Thinking of frostbite, and a change of subject, I take his hand to examine his fingers. "Where do they hurt?"

"It's not that," he says.

"Then what?"

He hesitates. "I lost my ring," he says. "My wedding band. I think it slipped off when I was getting out of the boat."

"Where? Near the shore?"

He nods.

"For God's sake." I duck out of the tent before he can stop me. I hear his voice behind me, asking me where I'm going, and I shout back, "Stay there."

I rush toward the water's edge, shivering in my still-damp clothes. The penguins purr as I go past, and a few of them scatter. I shine my flashlight down to the rocks at the bottom. I can't see much. I follow what I think was his path, sweeping the flashlight back and forth in front of me.

I'm in up to my knees when I see it—a flash of gold against the slate-colored rocks. I reach in, the water up to my shoulder, so cold it feels as if my arm will snap off and sink.

I manage to grasp the ring with fingers that now barely move, then shuffle back to shore on leaden feet. I hobble back to my own tent, where I strip off my clothes and don as many dry things as I can. My skin is moist and wrinkled from being wet for so long. I hear a noise and look up to see Dennis, blanket still wrapped around his shoulders, crouched at the opening to my tent.

"What are you staring at?" I snap. Then I look down to what he sees—a thin, faded T-shirt, no bra, my nipples pressing against the fabric, my arm flushed red from the cold. I pull his ring off my thumb and throw it at him.

He picks it up off the floor, holding it but not putting it on. "I wish you'd just left it," he says, almost to himself.

"A penguin could have choked on it," I say. "But no one ever thinks about that. We're all tourists here, you know. This is their home, not ours."

"I'm sorry," he says. "What can I do?"

I shake my head. He can't leave, which is the only thing I want him to do. There's nowhere for him to go.

He crawls into the tent, then pulls the blanket off his shoulders and places it around mine. He finds a fleece pullover in a pile of clothing and wraps it around my reddened arm.

"How cold is that water, anyway?" he asks.

"About thirty-five degrees, give or take." I watch him carefully.

"How long can someone survive in there?"

"Not very long," I say, remembering the expedition guide who'd drowned. He'd been trapped under the flipped Zodiac for only a few minutes but had lost consciousness, with rescuers only a hundred yards away. "You'd go into shock," I explain. "It's too cold to swim, even to breathe."

He unwraps my arm. "Does it feel better?"

"A little." Pain prickles my skin from the inside, somewhere deep down, and I feel an ache stemming from my bones. "You still haven't told me what you were doing out there."

Setting his ring to one side, he reaches over and begins massaging my arm. I'm not sure I want him to, but I know the warmth, the circulation, is good. "Like I said, I lost my ring."

"You were out much farther than the place I found your ring."

"I must have missed it." He doesn't look at me as he speaks. I watch his fingers on my arm, and I am reminded of the night before, when only Thom and I were here, and Thom had helped me wash my hair. The feel of his hands on my scalp, on my neck, had run through my entire body, tightening into a coil of desire that never fully vanished. But nothing has ever happened between Thom and me other than unconsummated rituals, generally toward the end of our stays. After a while touch becomes necessary, and we begin doing things for each other—he'll braid my long hair; I'll rub his feet.

Suddenly I pull away. I regard the stranger in my tent: his dark hair, streaked with silver; his sad, heavy eyes; his ringless hands, still outstretched.

"What's the matter?" he asks.

"Nothing."

"I was just trying to help." The tent's small lamp casts deep shadows under his eyes. "I'm sorry," he says. "I don't mean to cause you any trouble. I know you don't want me here."

Something in his voice softens the knot in my chest. I sigh. "I'm just not a people person, that's all."

For the first time, he smiles, barely. "I can see why you come here. Talk about getting away from it all."

"At least I leave when I'm supposed to," I say, offering a tiny smile of my own.

He glances down at Thom's clothing, pulled tight across his body. "So when do I have to leave?" he asks.

"They'll be here in the morning."

Then he says, "How's he doing? The guy who fell?"

It takes me a moment to realize what he's talking about. "I don't know," I confess. "I forgot to ask."

He leans forward, then whispers, "I know something about him."

"What's that?"

"He was messing around with that blond woman," he says. "The one who was right there when it happened. I saw you talking to her."

"How do you know?"

"I saw them. They had a rendezvous every night, on the deck, after his wife went to bed. The blonde was traveling with her sister. They even ate lunch together once, the four of them. The wife had no idea."

This is the type of story I normally can't tolerate, but I find myself intrigued. "Do you think they planned it?" I ask. "Or did they just meet, on the boat?"

"I don't know."

I look away, disappointed. "She seemed too young. For him."

"You didn't see her hands," he says. "My wife taught me that. You always know a woman's age by her hands. She may have had the face of a thirty-five-year-old, but she had the hands of a fifty-year-old."

"If you're married, why are you traveling alone?"

He pauses. "Long story."

"Well, we've got all night," I say.

"She decided not to come," he says.

"Why?"

"She left, a month ago. She's living with someone else."

"Oh." I don't know what more to say. Dennis is quiet, and I make another trip to the supply tent, returning with a half-empty bottle of brandy. His tired eyes brighten a bit.

He drinks down a couple of mouthfuls and hands the bottle back to me before speaking again. "She was seeing him for a long time," he says, "but I think it was this trip that set her off. She didn't want to spend three weeks on a boat with me, or without him."

"I'm sorry." A moment later, I ask, "Do you have kids?"

He nods. "Twin girls, in college. They don't call home much. I don't know if she's told them or not."

"Why did you decide to come anyway?"

"This trip was for our anniversary." He turns his head and gives me a cheerless smile. "Pathetic, isn't it?"

I roll the bottle slowly between my hands. "How did you lose the ring?"

"The ring?" He looks startled. "It just fell off, I guess."

"It was thirty degrees today. Weren't you wearing gloves?"

"I guess I wasn't."

I look at him, knowing there is more and that neither of us wants to acknowledge it. And then he lowers his gaze to my arm. "How does it feel?" he asks.

"It's okay."

"Let me work on it some more." He begins to rub my arm again. This time he slips his fingers inside the sleeves of my T-shirt, and the sudden heat on my skin seems to heighten my other senses: I hear the murmur of the penguins, feel the wind rippling the tent. At the same time, it's all drowned out by the feel of his hands.

I lean back and pull him with me until his head hovers just above mine. The lines sculpting his face look deeper in the tent's shadowy light, and his lazy eyelids lift as if to see me more clearly. He blinks, slowly, languidly, as I imagine he might touch me, and in the next moment he does.

I hear a pair of gentoos outside, their rattling voices rising above the night's ambient sound. Inside, Dennis and I move under and around our clothing, our own voices muted, whispered, breathless. In the sudden humid heat of the tent we've recognized each other in the same way as the penguins, by instinct, and, as with the birds, it's all we know.

During the Antarctic Night, tens of thousands of male emperors huddle together through a month of total darkness, in temperatures reaching seventy degrees below zero, as they incubate their eggs. By the time the females return to the colony, four months after they left, the males have lost half their body weight. They are near starvation, and yet they wait. It's what they're programmed to do.

Dennis does not wait for me. I wake up alone in my tent, the gray light of dawn nudging my eyelids. When I look at my watch, I see that it's later than I thought.

Outside, I glance around for Dennis, but he's not in camp. I make coffee, washing Thom's cup for him to use. I drink my own coffee without waiting for him; it's the only thing to warm me this morning, with him gone and the sun so well hidden.

I sip slowly, steam rising from my cup, and take in the moonscape around me: the edgy rocks, the mirrored water, ice sculptures rising above the pack ice—I could be on another planet. Yet for the first time in years, I feel as if I've reconnected with the world in some way, as if I am not as lost as I've believed all this time.

I hear the sound of a distant motor and stand up. Then it stops. I listen, hearing agitated voices—it must be Thom, coming from Palmer, having engine trouble. He is still outside the bay, out of sight, so I wait, washing my coffee mug and straightening up. When the engine starts up again, I turn back toward the bay. A few minutes later, Thom comes up from the shore with one of the electricians at Palmer, a young guy named Andy. I wave them over.

They walk hesitantly, and when they get closer, I recognize the look on Thom's face. Even before he opens his mouth, I know, with an icy certainty, where Dennis is.

"We found a body, Deb," he says. "In the bay." He exchanges a glance with Andy. "We just pulled him in."

I stare at their questioning faces. "He was here all night," I say. "I thought he just went for a walk, or—" I stop. Then I start toward the bay.

Thom steps in front of me. He holds both of my arms. "There's no need to do this," he says.

But I have to see for myself. I pull away and run toward the water's edge. The body lies across the rocks. I recognize Thom's sweater, stretched over Dennis's large frame.

I walk over to him; I want to take his pulse, to feel his heartbeat. But then I see his face, a bluish white, frozen in an expression I don't recognize, and I can't go any closer.

I feel Thom come up behind me. "It's him," I say. "I gave him your sweater."

He puts an arm around my shoulder. "What do you think happened?" he asks, but he knows as well as I do. There is no current in the bay, no way to be swept off this beach and pulled out to sea. The Southern Ocean is not violent here, but it is merciless nonetheless.

Antarctica is not a country; it is governed by an international treaty whose rules apply almost solely to the environment. There are no police, no firefighters, no medical examiners. We have to do everything ourselves, and I shrug Thom off when he tries to absolve me of our duties. I help them lift Dennis into the Zodiac, the weight of his body entirely different now. I keep a hand on his chest as we back out of the bay and speed away, as if he might suddenly try to sit up. When we arrive at Palmer, I finally give in, leaving others to the task of packing his body for its long journey home.

They offer me a hot shower and a meal. As Andy walks me down the hall toward the dormitory, he tries to find something to say. I'm silent, not helping him. Eventually he updates me on the injured man. "He's going to be okay," he tells me. "But you know what's strange? He doesn't remember anything about the trip. He knows his wife, knows who the president is, how to add two and two but he doesn't know how he got here, or why he even came to Antarctica. Pretty goddamned spooky, huh?"

He won't remember the woman he was fooling around with, I think. *She will remember him, but for him, she's already gone.*

Back at camp, I watch for the gentoos who lost their chick, but they do not return. Their nest remains abandoned, and other penguins steal their rocks.

Ten days later, Thom and I break camp and ready ourselves for the weeklong journey back. We have been working in a companionable near-silence, which is not entirely unusual. Our weeks together at the bottom of the earth have taught us the rhythms of each other's moods, and we don't always need to talk. We do not talk about Dennis.

Once on the boat, the distractions are many, and the hours and days disappear in seminars and lectures. The next thing I know, we are a day from the Drake Passage, the last leg of our journey, where the Southern Ocean, the Pacific Ocean, and the Atlantic all meet and toss boats around like toys. The tourists will get sick, and the smell of vomit will fill the halls, and I will take as much meclizine as I can stomach and stay in bed.

But today I wander the ship, walking the halls Dennis walked, sitting where he must have sat, standing where he may have stood. I'm with a new group of passengers now, none of whom would have crossed his path. A sleety rain begins to fall, and I go out to the upper deck. As we float through a labyrinth of icebergs, I play with Dennis's wedding ring, which he'd left on the floor of my tent. I wear it on my thumb, as I did when I first found it, because that's where it fits.

Because of the rain, I'm alone on the deck when I see it—a lone emperor penguin, sitting atop an enormous tabular iceberg. A good field guide would announce this sighting on the PA—the passengers aren't likely to get another chance to see an emperor. But I don't move; I watch her as she preens her feathers, and I imagine that she is feeling leisurely, safe, in a moment of peace she can't comprehend or enjoy.

They aren't aware of it, but the emperors' very survival depends on all but perfect timing. During the breeding season, the female must return from her journey within ten days of her chick's hatching. If she doesn't show, her partner, nearly dead from starvation, has no choice but to abandon their chick. He can't override his own instinctual will to live.

I believe that penguins mourn. I've seen Adélies wander their colonies, searching for mates that never return; I've seen chinstraps sitting dejected on empty nests. And I've seen the emperors grieve. The female returns, searching, her head poised for the ecstatic cry. When her calls go unanswered, she will lower her beak to the icy ground, where she will eventually find her chick, frozen in death, and she will assume the hunched posture of sorrow as she wanders across the ice.

THE ROAD TO HANA

Again they're arguing even before they leave the hotel. Ethan lets the door shut behind him, and Sue contemplates staying. Let him get to their rental car, start the engine, and wait. Or would he leave the resort, hit the Piilani Highway, and head off to Hana without her? Perhaps she shouldn't test his loyalty, not today.

Still, she lingers for a few moments, just long enough to make a point. She wanders through the oversized suite, checking that the lights are off, the hair dryer unplugged, a luxury she does not have at home as she ushers their two teenagers out of the house and wonders later, standing in the kitchen of a new property with a client, whether her own stove is off. She pours a glass of water and drinks half of it, then finally pockets her key card and goes downstairs.

The hotel's open-air lobby is overflowing with palms, and she doesn't see Ethan until she recognizes his impatient wave from the car.

"Do you have the camera?" she asks as they merge onto the two-lane highway.

"Yes."

She looks at him. His eyes are on the road, his jaw set. "Let's just forget I ever mentioned anything, okay?" she says, referring to their argument.

"I'd like to," he says.

"Then why can't you? We're here to celebrate our anniversary, for God's sake. Besides, what happened with the ring was thirty-odd years ago. It didn't have anything to do with you."

"I think it does."

"It's just a ring, Ethan. And it's not as if another man gave it to me or anything."

This elicits a humorless laugh. "I think I would actually prefer *that*," he says.

She sighs and turns to look out the window. "Do you know how to get there?"

"Vaguely. The map's in the side pocket, in the guidebook." He nods toward the passenger door.

She pulls it out, opens it up, and studies the zigzag of lines representing the road to Hana. "Listen to this," she says. "'The Hana Highway is fifty miles long. Thanks to its hairpin turns, blind curves, and the eight-to ten-hour day it entails, the Road to Hana is often called the Road to Divorce by couples who dare to embark upon it.'"

She catches his eye, timing it just right. They both begin to laugh.

"Let's stop in Paia for breakfast," she suggests. "We'll need our strength."

"Okay," he says. "Whatever you want."

She leans over and kisses his ear. He turns toward her, and she pulls away. "Eyes on the road!" she says.

"Relax. We haven't even reached the hairy part yet."

He's right: Sue looks at the map and sees that the serious zigzags start after Twin Falls. She hopes it's not as bad as it looks.

Along Paia's strip of surf shops and seaside cafés, they walk past windows awash with surfing gear and beachwear until they encounter the only restaurant that's open—a hot, cramped café, five of its six tables full, its air moist and redolent with brown sugar.

After they order, he leans back in his chair. "So, did you bring it with you?" he asks.

She looks at him, surprised. "Why?"

"Just wondering. I didn't see it in the safe when I put my laptop in."

"I don't want to start another fight."

"I know," he says. "Let me see it."

She touches the ring, which is in the front pocket of her shorts. "Promise you won't get mad?"

He nods.

She takes it out and holds it between her fingers for a moment—an intricately designed ring, probably an antique, of white gold, with five meager diamonds enveloped in its flowery arcs and swirls. She hands it to him.

He holds it up, inspecting it. "I can't believe you brought it with you."

"I still don't see why it upsets you."

He places the ring on the table, between them.

"I was in high school, for God's sake," she says. "Until a few weeks ago, I completely forgot I had it."

Their meals arrive, enormous plates of fruit and eggs and potatoes for which Sue suddenly has little appetite. She picks at chunks of pineapple and lifts her eyes to watch Ethan eat. He holds his fork, as always, with his fingers over the top; he sips his coffee while still chewing. Twenty years of marriage, of sitting across the breakfast table from this man, and she still can't quite grow accustomed to his habits.

Yet as far as bad habits go, Ethan has few, though his reaction to the ring had come as a surprise. At this point in their marriage, Ethan doesn't notice, or even pretend to notice, a new suit or haircut; even a change of hair color hadn't registered when she finally covered her increasingly stubborn strands of gray. But for some reason, the night before, he detected the ring immediately when she slipped it on as they were heading out for dinner. Perhaps it was because they were away from home, or because it was their anniversary—for whatever reason, the ring seized his attention, even before the new dress or the updo that had taken her half an hour to perfect.

Ethan reached for her hand. *I've never seen this before.*

It's old, she said. *I've had it since I was a kid.*

It doesn't look like a kid's ring. Where'd you get it?

Don't worry, she said. *It's not a gift from a secret lover. I'll tell you over dinner.*

Yet, at the restaurant, she had waited for the wine before she began and then paused to order an appetizer. She found something strangely exotic in the telling, or rather just before the telling—in the promise of having a story, one that had nothing to do with their daughters and their tennis and softball schedules or with the school board. It had nothing to do with the latest software launch at Ethan's company, or with Sue's dwindling real-estate commissions—it was simply a tale about herself, long ago, during a time when she was not yet defined by her work or her marriage or her children. It was astonishing to her that she'd forgotten about the ring, which she'd discovered in a long-sealed box while cleaning out the storage room a few months earlier. It was even more astonishing, and somehow thrilling, that after more than twenty years of life with Ethan, she was about to tell him a story that he'd never heard before.

And so she had wanted to prolong the feeling of being mysterious, this undercurrent of excitement that normally eluded them, even when they did manage solo evenings out together. And then, after she told him, a new, dreadful sense of mystery filled her: the wonder of how, after decades with this man, she could have so horribly misjudged his reaction.

"Aren't you going to eat anything?" Ethan interrupts her thoughts, indicating her plate. Her breakfast is still untouched.

She shakes her head. "I guess I'm not as hungry as I thought I was."

"Well, like you said, we need our strength."

"You know, it's just a piece of jewelry," she says.

Ethan sets his fork across his empty plate. "Jewelry always means something."

"Not when you're a kid."

"Sure it does. I read about a girl who escaped from North Korea— she bought her way out, with her mother's bracelets. Now she's safe, she lives in the States, but she still wears dozens of bracelets on her arms. She's afraid to take them off—she thinks she might need them again. For her, they mean freedom."

"That's different, obviously."

"You've kept the ring all these years," he says. "It must mean something to you."

She checks her watch. "We should get back on the road."

As they cross to the eastern side of the island, the sun ducks behind rain clouds, and large drops intermittently hit the windshield. Ethan turns up the radio, masking the silence in the car.

Sue had put the ring back in her pocket. She'd brought it with her this morning thinking that maybe she could leave it at one of the stops on the Road to Hana, for someone to discover. Perhaps instead she should toss it into the sea. She feels the need for a ceremonial parting.

She remembers when Brooke Wheeler first wore it to school, during their junior year. It was an heirloom, from her grandmother, a gift for Brooke's sixteenth birthday. It was huge on Brooke's tiny, graceful hand. All the girls, including Sue, coveted the ring, which Brooke twirled around her finger in study hall and gazed upon in class.

Sue hadn't had a chance to try it on, as many of the other girls had; she wasn't a friend of Brooke's and could never have hoped to be. The two had gym class together, but Brooke had never acknowledged her. Then, one morning just before class, when Brooke took off her ring before volleyball, Sue watched her leave it on the wooden bench in the locker room, so preoccupied with her friends, her hair, that she apparently forgot all about it. Alone in the locker room, Sue picked it up. She turned to follow Brooke to the court; she would return the ring, become a hero, and never again be ignored by Brooke and her coterie. Then she changed her mind. If she returned it later, after Brooke had panicked and searched and mourned its loss, she would be an even bigger hero.

Nearly giddy with the thought, she stashed it in her locker and joined the class. She snuck glances at Brooke, who was laughing with her friends, unaware of what she'd lost. It wasn't until after they'd all showered and changed and Brooke went to don the ring that she discovered it was gone. Then came a loud shriek, a rush of girls on their hands and knees, a trip to the principal's office to report it missing.

Sue helped in the search, though Brooke hadn't seemed to notice. Sue and her best friend, Maria, talked about it at lunch, by which time Brooke was offering a reward.

Probably the janitor will find it, Sue said. *I'm sure it just fell into a crack somewhere.*

Right, Maria scoffed. *Whoever stole it will probably be the one to "find" it. Brooke may be dumb, but she's not stupid.*

Sue regarded her friend, her only friend, a girl as plump as Sue was skinny, as outspoken as Sue was quiet, and just as invisible. Fear rose in Sue's throat, and she pushed her sandwich away. *Well, she couldn't prove anything.*

Maybe she could. I heard both her parents are lawyers.

It was the first secret she'd kept from Maria, the first moment she realized how her life would be different with secrets.

She looks out the rain-spotted window of the car, at the odd angles of light falling between the clouds. The radio station emits occasional static, but neither she nor Ethan bothers to change stations. She turns from the window to regard her husband, the morning's quarrel still reverberating in her head.

What else are you keeping from me, Sue? he'd asked when he saw the ring on the nightstand, where she'd carelessly tossed it after their argument the night before.

She had laughed out loud. *This again? Come on, Ethan.*

I'm serious, he said. *I can't believe you could do something like this to someone and not think it's a big deal.*

Sue, with a lighthearted air she didn't feel, brushed aside his concern. *Don't be ridiculous,* she said. He only looked back at her, apparently still waiting for an answer. *Okay,* she added. *I swear to you, this is the only evil thing I've ever done in my whole life. Now you know everything.*

Do I?

She tilted her head. *Why are you looking for a reason to fight with me?* she asked. *Is there something you want to say to me?*

He glanced away, and she leaned forward. *That's it, isn't it? Come on, out with it.*

But he only told her that if they wanted to make it to Hana they'd better hurry up.

The night Sue had stolen the ring, it had gone into a sock at the bottom of her dresser drawer. She switched the ring's home several times, so that none of her socks would go unworn; her mother tended to notice things like that. Sue grew accustomed to living with the fear of discovery, with the headaches and insomnia that went along with it. She wanted more than anything to undo what she'd done, but she couldn't see any way out.

Yet the ring had given her something that eventually eclipsed the fear and regret—a sense of confidence, of *power,* a sense that if she could get away with this, she could do anything. Sometimes, during the many nights when sleep eluded her, she would take the ring out and slide it onto her finger, imagining it belonged there. The weight of it on her hand had a soporific effect; she would close her eyes and relax into the subtle calm that preceded sleep. And at the same time, as if her body knew better, she would awaken just before dawn, with enough time to take the ring off and hide it again before her mother's knock at the door.

With no other way out, she began to convince herself that she *deserved* the ring, that it was fair compensation. Brooke had been given more than she had: beauty, wealth, the easy confidence that went along with both. With Brooke's ring ensconced in her drawer, Sue felt as if she were finally an equal, and one day she found the courage to approach Brooke on the volleyball court, compliment her on her serve, and ask for tips.

Brooke invited her to lunch that day, and as Sue followed them through the cafeteria, she would not allow her eyes to rest on Maria, sitting alone at their usual spot. It was a surprisingly easy transition, after so many years of longing, but there was no salvation in it. She quickly discovered that she was not the only one with a secret; every girl had something hidden away, though not from everyone. As Sue learned of the kisses stolen from one another's boyfriends and the origins of false rumors making their way through the school, she realized that every one of them lived a precarious social existence, their friendships balanced on the sharp edge of an inherent distrust. She soon wished to return to the long empty table she'd shared with Maria, to the safety, if not the glamour, of having one trusted, unpopular friend. But by then she could not find her way back.

Her stomach rumbles, the sound drowned by the music in the car. Sue opens the guidebook to look for a place to stop. Ethan was right; she should have eaten breakfast—now she is starving when he is full, and if she eats now, she'll be full when he gets hungry. When freed of the kids and their schedules, they are no longer in synch.

She glances over at him, his eyes on the road, the previously tense look now melted into his features, rounded with middle-aged pounds—

which, she has noticed lately, have also been melting. She could feel, the other night when she joined him in the shower, that he is thinner, firmer than usual. *Have you been losing weight?* she murmured into his neck.

He seemed nervous, self-conscious. *Don't I wish.*

She pulled away to study him. *If you haven't been trying, maybe there's something wrong.*

Nothing's wrong, he said, irritated.

I only meant it as a compliment, she said, then realized that the weight might have been coming off steadily for months and she just hadn't noticed. Making love wasn't as it used to be—heated and insatiable and curious—but was now hurried, dark, mechanical, if it happened at all. Surely this is only natural when busy, dual-career couples have teenagers. When else do you find the time, except in the middle of the night, in the shadows of the master bedroom, in the sleepy haze of those precious hours past your kids' curfew but before your alarm sounds?

Sue lowers the volume to read Ethan a paragraph about Twin Falls. "Two waterfalls," she says, "and a lagoon we can swim in. Glad we wore our suits."

"Where's the turnoff?"

"At the two-mile marker, it says."

"Two-mile marker?" he says. "Where did the Road to Hana actual-ly start?"

"I haven't the foggiest."

"Well, what else does it say?"

"There's a place to park, right by a sign that says NO PARKING."

"That's helpful."

She looks up from the guidebook, then grabs his arm. "There it is! Turn there."

He brakes abruptly and swerves onto a gravel turnoff, sending her head crashing into his shoulder. "Ouch," she says, and rubs her temple.

A couple of cars are parked to the right, with space for one more. Af-ter Ethan maneuvers into the spot, Sue gets out and stretches. "Looks like we've got the place to ourselves," she says.

The trail's beginning is wide and flat, a dirt road surrounded by a verdant, leafy jungle. After about ten minutes, they reach a fork, where Ethan looks at her expectantly. "Which way?"

"I don't know."

"Check the guidebook."

"It's in the car." She holds up a hand to cut off his next comment before he can get it out. "It's too heavy to carry around. We don't need it. I think it's this way."

They follow the dirt path, whose trees and shrubs close in until the path simply ends. They can't walk any further without a machete.

Ethan curses under his breath and turns around. Sue is surprised, as she has been recently, at how quick he is to impatience and frustration. She remembers, shortly before they left, taking him aside in the kitchen one evening after he'd barked at their younger daughter at dinner. He blamed his recent schedule, the toll of late nights at work, the lack of good sleep. *We're all swamped*, she reminded him. *The girls and I don't take it out on you.* He'd given her a long, wide-eyed look. He opened his mouth as if to say something, then seemed to change his mind. He apologized to her and to their daughter and then went to bed, hours early.

"What's the big rush, Ethan?" she says now.

"We don't have much time here if you want to go all the way to Hana."

"So we don't make it all the way to Hana," she says. "So what?"

He shrugs. "Fine by me."

They reach the crossroads again and set out on the other path, which also quickly narrows, the vegetation closing in on them, exposing only the ground under their feet and patches of sky above. As Sue observes the imprints Ethan's shoes leave in the moist earth, and her own next to his, she suddenly feels she is limited to a certain destiny, that this shrinking trail is leading nowhere she especially wants to go.

The trail slickens into smooth round rocks and mud, then narrows further to nothing more than an elevated wall. They hear the rush of water in the distance. Sue holds her arms out for balance and avoids looking down at the sharp points of rocks below.

They reach a small pool whose waterfall is not much more than a trickle. "Let's keep going," Sue says quickly. She moves past Ethan and takes the lead, stepping carefully on the slimy tree roots, her shoes occasionally sliding into the muck below.

She stops when she sees that her next step hovers above water—a clear greenish pool fanning out before a gushing waterfall. "We made it," she says, relieved. They are completely alone, more alone than she

has felt in a long time, and, at the moment, something about their solitude feels forbidden.

On a large flat rock, she begins to pull off her clothes. As she steps
out of her shorts, she hears a *clink*. She reaches down to where the
ring has fallen, amazed that she'd managed to forget about it. Once un-
dressed down to her suit, she lets the ring drop next to her clothing. As
she enters the water, she looks back and sees it winking beside her T-
shirt.

Ethan has stripped down to his trunks but is still standing on the
rock, taking photos. Sue lowers her face into the water, her eyes skim-
ming the surface, and watches him. When he joins her in the pool, she
swims over to him, wrapping her legs around his waist. She leans in to
kiss him, but he's leaning away.

"What's with you?" she asks.

He doesn't answer.

"You've been acting strange ever since we got here," she says. "And
don't tell me it's that stupid ring."

He looks at her, the same wide, steady gaze he'd given her in the
kitchen that night. "You're right. It's not the ring," he says.

She shrinks away from him. As he begins to speak, she lets her face
sink into the pool again, half-hearing his muted words as the water fills
her ears. She watches his mouth, as if she can see the words form and
drift into the air, hovering there in the late-morning light; she wants
them to stay there, to prevent them from swimming into her ears, being
processed by her brain—but a part of her knows, in fact fully compre-
hends, what he is saying. A part of her has known it all along.

"You're a bastard," she says.

"I'm sorry," he says. "I've been trying to find a way to tell you for
months. There's no such thing as a 'good time' for this."

"Did you have to pick the worst?" She feels tears rising and quickly ducks under the water, to rinse them away. "Have you talked to her
since we've been here? Do you call her every day?"

He turns toward the rocks. "I think we should go."

"What else do you think?" she shouts after him. "Do you think you're
in love with her? Do you think you want to leave me and the girls?"

She watches his body still, his back motionless in the water until it
bends slightly toward her. "I didn't say that. I didn't say I wanted that."

"Then what?"

Then he puts his fingers to his lips and points toward the path. Sue looks up to see another couple entering the clearing. She isn't sure whether they heard anything, but she doubts it; they're young, probably in their twenties, arm in arm, faces bent together, lips never far apart.

Just then, they notice Sue and Ethan, obviously surprised to discover that they, too, are not alone. "Hi," the young woman calls out. "Hope we're not disturbing you. We didn't know anyone else was here."

Ethan doesn't answer. "Not at all," Sue says.

"I'm Lori," the young woman says, "and this is my husband, Jeff." She giggles. "I can't get used to saying that," she confesses. "We're on our honeymoon."

"Congratulations," says Sue.

"You don't mind if we join you?" Jeff asks, taking possession of the rock next to the one on which Sue and Ethan have left their clothes, the only one not green with moss.

"We were just leaving," Ethan says.

"Yes, we'll be leaving in a little while," Sue says. He gives her an insistent look, and she relishes his irritation. "One last swim, and then we're continuing to Hana."

"That's where we're going, too," says Lori, "though we haven't exactly been on schedule so far."

"This is worth the stop," Sue says. "Come on in. The water's beautiful."

As Lori and Jeff prepare to enter the pool, Ethan turns to her and hisses, "Sue, let's go. Now."

She whispers back, "You can't have everything you want, Ethan."

"Well, I'm leaving."

"Go ahead. I'll meet you at the car."

He climbs up to their rock and pulls on his shirt. The water on his back soaks through, leaving big dark spots. They'd forgotten to bring towels.

Sue turns away from him to greet Lori and Jeff, who have stepped into the water but remain joined at the waist, hands, shoulders. She realizes then that she really should be leaving with Ethan, at the very least to give these kids their privacy, but having made a bit of a scene she can't do it just yet. She looks over to see her husband's back disappear into the rainforest.

She can tell by the faces of her new companions that the tension between Ethan and herself has not gone unnoticed. "I'm sorry about that," she says. "We're having a—a disagreement. Not really the sort of thing young people like you want to see on your honeymoon."

"It's no problem," Jeff says charitably.

"Yeah," Lori says, "it's totally okay. Nothing can spoil our mood."

Sue is reminded of her older daughter, who at seventeen is madly in love with the water polo captain at her high school, and she wonders whether all young love is the same, whether they all believe, as she once did, that nothing can mar it.

"Want to join us for lunch?" Jeff asks. He indicates a picnic basket on the rocks, next to their clothing. "The hotel packed it for us—there's a ton of food, way more than we could eat."

With his invitation, the hunger inside Sue reawakens. It's impossible, she knows, to be thinking of food when she's just received the most devastating news of her married life—but there it is, a hunger gnawing in her gut, a sudden emptiness aching to be filled. And she doesn't care about making Ethan wait.

"I'd love to," she says. "If you wouldn't mind."

"Of course not!" Lori says. She leads the way to the basket, and together they lay out the food: sandwiches, pasta salad, fruit, brownies. They chat about the island, the weather, the sights seen and still to be seen. Sue begins to relax in their presence. Their happiness is so complete, the nature of their love so uncomplicated, she begins to forget about her own troubles. She wishes she could stay with them all day, all the way to Hana, to see the wonder of its scenery through their eyes instead of through her own.

But soon Lori looks at her watch and stands up. As Lori reaches for her towel, Sue gathers the linen cloth they'd spread out in front of them and begins to pack the plastic dishes and leftover food. Sue hears a splash and glances over her shoulder to see that Jeff is taking another dip in the pool.

"You'll be all wet in the car," Lori calls out to him from the rock, where she is putting on her clothes. He doesn't hear, or ignores her, and she looks at Sue. "Are all men so stubborn?"

"I don't know about all," Sue says, pulling on her shorts, "but I know my husband is."

Lori watches Jeff for a moment, then asks, "Is the first year really the most difficult?"

Surprised, Sue pauses, hands reaching into the sleeves of her T-shirt. "Actually, I think it was the easiest, looking back. In reality, it was probably the most fun. The big challenges come later, when you have kids and have to try to keep up with them and your house and your job and everything else." She stops, then smiles. "Not to worry, honey. It's all good stuff. You'll see."

"I hope so," Lori says, so quietly that Sue almost misses it.

Jeff emerges from the pool, and a few minutes later, with Jeff in the lead, they start back toward the parking lot together, passing couples and families along the trail. Occasionally Jeff turns back to warn Lori and Sue of bulging tree roots or slippery rocks.

In the parking lot, Sue helps them pack up their car. She glances over at Ethan, sitting in the driver's seat of their own rental car with the door open. She sees the guidebook open and propped on the steering wheel, though she doubts he is reading.

Sue impulsively gives Lori and Jeff each a hug. "Thanks for lunch," she says. "Have a great trip to Hana. Enjoy the rest of your honeymoon." She watches them get into their car and drive away. Then she joins Ethan.

He turns the car around and pauses at the mouth of the lot. "Which way?" he asks quietly.

She looks at her watch: only a few hours of daylight left. They wouldn't make it even halfway to Hana before dark. "Let's go just a little further," she says. She pages through the guidebook. "Here. There's a small town up ahead. We could see just a little bit more before we go all the way back."

They drive in silence; like the trail to the falls, the road narrows and curves, and they traverse it as carefully as they had earlier, pulling over and stopping when the road recedes to one lane, letting a parade of cars pass before tooting the horn and continuing on.

Sue's seatbelt has twisted across her hips, and she is trying to smooth it out when suddenly she stops and clutches her pockets. "The ring," she says. She turns both pockets inside out. "It's gone."

"What?" Instinctively, Ethan slows down.

"I must've left it at the waterfall." She thinks back, seeing its sparkling

light from the pool—and then? She doesn't remember seeing it again
after that, but then she wasn't thinking about it.

They've stopped at the beginning of a blind curve, and Ethan waves to
the driver behind them to go around. "Do you want me to go back?"

She sighs, thinking about it. "No," she says. "There's really no point,
is there?"

Sue points to the left, toward a long row of mailboxes. "Turn there."

He flips on the left turn signal and waits. The traffic returning from
Hana, heavy and slow, doesn't ease up. Sue watches the approaching
cars, examining the faces behind each windshield, mostly couples. She
wonders about them: how long they've been together, whether they
love each other, whether one of them, or both, loves someone else.
Finally, one of the cars stops to let them turn.

"Thank you!" she calls through her open window, then is surprised
to see that it's Jeff and Lori, on their way back already. They didn't
make it very far either, Sue thinks. Lori seems to recognize them at the
same moment, and she lifts her hand to wave. That's when Sue sees it:
the silvery flash of the ring, her ring, on Lori's right hand, unmistakable
in the late afternoon light. Sue's mouth opens—but she has no words
for what she sees.

Lori catches her mistake and lowers her hand. The two women's eyes
lock. So this is it, Sue thinks, this is the new fate of Brooke's ring. As
Ethan makes the turn and as Jeff and Lori continue on their way, Sue
watches the ring disappear, passing again from one woman to another,
from one generation to the next, cementing its legacy of longing.

Ethan hadn't noticed Jeff and Lori, or the ring. "Well, we're here,"
he says, glancing around as they drive along a gravelly dirt road. "What
now?"

"It doesn't matter," she says. "Maybe we should head back."

As if reading her mind, he doesn't ask why but simply turns around.
Sue rubs her hands together, the right bare, the left still wearing her
wedding band—for how much longer, she can't know. She and Ethan
join the line of cars returning from Hana, each one close behind the
other, traveling carefully from one blind curve to the next.

FORGETTING ENGLISH

Tell me your birth day and year," Jing-wei says. When Paige tells her, Jing-wei writes them down. They are sitting in a Taipei McDonald's, across from the language school where Paige teaches. Today, Paige is the student. It is their first meeting.

"You were born in the Year of the Tiger," Jing-wei tells her a moment later. "It's my hobby, the Chinese zodiac," she explains. "Next time, I can tell you about your future and who you should choose as your husband. *You mei you nan pengyou?* Do you have boyfriend in America?"

Paige shakes her head. "I just want to learn numbers," she says, "and how to read street signs and menus."

Jing-wei nods, her long, layered hair brushing her shoulders. She opens a Chinese textbook, then points to a column of characters. She recites the numbers, then asks Paige to do the same. As practice, Jing-wei asks her how much she paid for her breakfast, her bus fare. She asks what Paige's wages are, how much she weighs. Then she says, without a hint of irony, "Can I ask personal question?"

Paige hesitates. "Well. Okay."

"*Ni ji sui*? How old are you?"

Paige looks at the textbook to find the number. "*San shi,*" she says: thirty. Too old, she knows, to be starting over like this, and when she looks at Jing-wei, she feels even older. She doesn't ask but guesses that Jing-wei is in her early twenties.

They continue the lesson, Jing-wei asking in her soft, clear voice how long Paige has been in Taipei, how much she paid for her blouse. By the end of their session, Paige can count to ten. Progress. They arrange to meet again.

As she waits for the bus back to her apartment, Paige gazes across the street at the neon lights, the blinking red characters over restaurants, on billboards. She studies them hopefully, wondering if one day she might be able to decipher them, if one day she might be able to translate the jumble of her own life into something coherent. As she waits, she practices the numbers, repeating the strange words—*yi, er, san, si, wu, liu, qi, ba, jiu, shi*—over and over, softly, as if murmuring a prayer.

"Why don't you change your shirt?" asks her roommate, Abbey, indicating Paige's long sleeves.

"The heat doesn't bother me," Paige says, as a bead of sweat runs down the middle of her back.

Abbey is a British expatriate whose previous roommate abruptly left the country just before Paige arrived. *Couldn't handle it,* Abbey told her. *Don't understand it, really. Twenty hours of teaching per week, at four hundred kuai an hour—what's not to like?* She shook her head. *The waiguoren here are so spoiled they don't even know it.*

The apartment is plain—a desk, two chairs, a coffee table, a television—and its tiled floors are clammy beneath Paige's feet. The walls are a worn off-white, with a long crack snaking down one of them, from the 1999 earthquake three years earlier. Sliding doors open onto a narrow balcony muffled with hanging plants, and a moldy clothesline sways above the doorway. A fan on the desk swirls the hot air and the ashes from Abbey's cigarettes.

Abbey lights another cigarette and tosses the pack onto the coffee table before propping her feet there. "So," she says, "you've never actually told me what brought you to Taiwan. A bit far from Chicago, isn't it, really?"

Paige picks up the pack, a Chinese brand, and pretends to inspect it. Abbey waits for an answer, and Paige puts the cigarettes down and shrugs. In truth, she hadn't done much research. She left suddenly, and it didn't matter where she went, as long as the money was decent. First she looked at what countries were farthest away; then she looked for work—jobs requiring few references and no specific skills. Asia was the most viable all around, and she liked Taiwan, especially once she saw it on a map: a mere droplet between the Pacific Ocean and China Sea—a small, leaf-shaped island drifting away from China's massive shadow.

✧

At the language school, she catches the other American teacher, Gabe, staring at her long sleeves. She turns away, trying to ignore him. Later, after classes, he invites her to grab a bite at a nearby night market. Paige demurs, having seen him leave after work with several different women, all teachers.

He keeps asking, and she keeps returning home alone to the stifling apartment, where she swallows the thick, smoky air and drinks can after can of Taiwan Beer. She grades her students' homework, listening to Abbey talk and sometimes taking a toke from her hash pipe, until they both grow heavy-lidded and head to their rooms. There Paige lies awake, listening to the rumble of traffic, the rain on the windows, the neighborhood kids setting off firecrackers in the alleys. She inevitably gets up for a walk, in hopes of seducing sleep. She often finds the streets slick from recent rain, reflecting the ubiquitous neon lights. The summery scent of wet asphalt makes her forget where she is until she catches a whiff of *chou doufu*, stinky tofu, from the vendor down the block.

Tonight, she walks all the way to the harbor. The sky is cloudy and starless, the water murky and dull, and she breathes in dank, fishy odors, magnified by the humid air. It is the only time she feels at home here, camouflaged by the darkness that masks the white of her skin and the red of her hair. It is the only time she can almost relax, with another day behind her, and the next one still hours away.

It's the little things she finds most exhausting: reading a map, asking a question, buying a bag of noodles. The language reminds her of how far away she is; words hiss and snap in her ears, achingly unfamiliar, and on the streets she feels both safe from and deprived of human contact.

So the next evening, when Gabe asks her yet again to the night market, she agrees, longing for the simplicity and comfort of having someone order her food. After class, she follows him into the gluey night air. They turn into a dim alley. At the end, light blanches the street, forming a halo over the short concrete buildings that evoke an overcrowded cemetery.

Gabe has lived in Taipei for three years, and he was born in the Year of the Rat. She knows little else about him, and he knows less about her. He doesn't know that last year she made six figures, that she gave it up for the twelve dollars an hour she makes here. He doesn't know that she sold everything she owned and left for Taipei without a word to anyone. He doesn't know that she's been on her own since she was seventeen.

They walk in silence, passing long tables displaying packages of men's, women's, and children's underwear; hair accessories; cheap jewelry; Hello Kitty notebooks, pencils, and pens; Chinese books and magazines. In the food stalls, fried dumplings sizzle in oil and various meats sear on grills, constantly flipped and slathered with sauces by sweaty cooks.

As they approach a man holding a live snake, Gabe finally speaks. "Have you tried the snake?" he asks.

The snake, upside down, writhes in the air. "Tried as in *eaten?* No."

"Watch," Gabe says. "He's going to cut off the head, then drain the blood and make a soup. It's incredibly good for your health. Plus it's an aphrodisiac."

"I thought we were just having dinner," she says.

He laughs but doesn't answer, keeping his eyes on the man with the snake, who snips off the head with a pair of large scissors, then squeezes it from the top, as if it were a tube of toothpaste. Blood slowly fills a jar. Paige looks away.

Gabe hands her a tiny opaque cup filled with dark liquid. "It's mixed with *kaoliang*," he says. "It'll kill the taste of the blood."

She takes a tentative sip. It tastes of rubbing alcohol. They sit on grimy metal chairs to eat. She watches Gabe pluck a chunk of snake from his bowl with chopsticks and pull its meat from the bones, revealing a tiny rib cage. She watches his tousled blond hair tumble into his eyes.

They finish and start walking again. When they reach the end of the night market, they turn the corner, into a darker, quieter alley.

"Don't you have any short-sleeved shirts?" he asks, with a hesitant smile. "For these sultry Taipei nights?"

"It's late," she says. "I should get home." But she doesn't move as he reaches for her hand. She lets him reach down and pick up her arm, unbutton the cuff, and roll up the sleeve. She lets him look at her scars, stark and grotesque in the dim alley.

He runs a finger lightly over her wrist. "Does it hurt?" he asks.

"No." The surface of the skin is dead, but underneath, somewhere deep down, she feels twinges of pain, the sensation of flesh knitting itself back together, the promise of healing. Yet the outside is still mottled and ugly, a dark purple against her pale skin.

He walks her to the bus stop. She leaves her sleeve rolled up, feeling for the first time Taipei's hot night air against her skin. His muted reaction to her scars came without judgment, without anything but a strange, endearing curiosity. And so she lets him kiss her while they wait for the bus, his hands on her face, in her long, tangled hair.

When the bus arrives, they ignore it. He hails a cab, which takes them to his apartment, a small box above a noisy banquet hall. Inside, not a single sensation escapes her: the heat of his body, the lumps in his bed, the sounds of the city below, the smell of peanut oil and garlic in the air. She feels herself reawakening from a dark, dreamless sleep, so fully that it takes her breath away, her body's reaction astonishing in its metamorphosis from pain, and numbness, to pleasure, sweet and fierce at once.

At her next lesson, Paige learns the Chinese word for "sad."

"*Shang xin*," she repeats.

"*Shang* means 'to wound,'" Jing-wei explains. "*Xin* means 'heart,' so *shang xin* means 'wounded heart.'" Jing-wei studies her a moment. "You are like typical Tiger," she adds softly. "Tigers are very moody. But this is the Year of the Horse, you know. Horse year is a very turbulent year—sometimes good, sometimes bad. For you, for Tiger, it's a year of freedom—because horses like to roam." Jing-wei pokes at the ice in her cup with her straw. "I was born in the Year of the Snake, you know. For Snake, Horse Year is not good. Horses are afraid of snakes— snakes make them jump. It can bring very bad things—bad for romance, bad for health."

"Maybe you shouldn't focus on bad things."

"This is Water Horse Year," Jing-wei continues, "and I was born under the fire sign. This will create boiling. Relationships can suffer. For me, it is my family. My parents want me to take my father's business.

You see, they had six daughters before me. I was last chance for boy. So I have more pressure than my sisters. They want me to study very hard."

"They expect you to study all the time?" Paige asks.

"Oh, yes," Jing-wei says. "I have boyfriend, but they do not know. They would never approve. My parents are very—how to say, old-fashion? One of my sisters got married last year, and her husband was not her choice. But she says she would rather have her husband tell her what to do than her father."

Jing-wei leans forward and scribbles some Chinese characters on a sheet of paper. "Look," she says. "In Chinese, to say you marry is different than in English. In English, you say, 'I marry him,' or 'I marry her.' But in Chinese, when a girl gets married, she says, *Jia gei le ta*, and that means 'I give him home.' When a boy gets married, he says, *Qu le ta*, meaning 'I take her.'"

"Really?"

Jing-wei nods. "My parents think this way, very traditional." She sighs. "*Wo de nan pengyou shi Meiguoren.* You understand? My boyfriend is American. My parents will never accept him."

Paige thinks of Steven. Her friends never knew about him. Nor did any of her colleagues, or his wife.

"I think we are supposed to find each other and be together," Jing-wei says. "We call it *yuan fen*—our fate. Do you believe?"

Paige shakes her head. "Not really."

"I can teach you many Chinese beliefs," Jing-wei says. She opens one of the books she brought with her. "Do you know that we have Ghost Month now?"

"You mean like Hallowe'en?" Paige asks. "In America, kids dress up in costumes and go from house to house collecting candy."

"In Taiwan, we feed the ghosts, not the children," Jing-wei says. "We leave food and drinks at temple, and burn ghost money, because during this month all the spirits come back to earth."

Paige thinks of the temple near her apartment; she has noticed the table of food, the thicker smoke, but she hadn't realized what it was for.

"You need to make the ghosts happy," Jing-wei explains, "or they will bring bad luck."

She lets a smile invade her lips, until she sees Jing-wei's expression.

"You're serious?"

"Even scientists believe," Jing-wei insists. "They offer food to the souls of animals they use for research. It is most important to pray for the spirits who don't have anyone to care for them."

"I see," Paige says.

"You must be careful during Ghost Month," Jing-wei says. "It's very bad time to get married, or to make business, or to move to new house. If you move, the spirits of your relatives may not be able to find their home, and they will take revenge."

Paige remembers the night she cut herself; she saw no white light, felt no spiritual reawakening. It remains, for her, an unemotional event, a physical injury from which she recovered and moved on.

Yet on her way home that evening, as she passes her neighborhood temple, she pauses and peeks inside. No one is around, but the enormous urn spouts thick gray smoke. The table is laden with fruit and candy, cans and bottles, and two steaming plates of food. Paige holds a vegetable *baozi* in her hand, which she bought for dinner from the vendor on the corner. After a surreptitious glance around, she scoots into the temple and pulls it from its paper bag. She sets it down, then hurries back outside.

Paige realizes, as she watches the procession make its way to the water, that she shouldn't have gotten stoned with Abbey before going to Ghost Month's Chung Yuan festival. Abbey had been too far gone to get off the couch, so Paige now walks alone through the crowds, lights, and smoke to see the floats and candlelit lanterns of the ceremonies. It will be another two weeks before the gates of hell close again, ending the spirits' roaming.

Heading toward the harbor, she feels disoriented but doesn't want to turn back. She passes a temple and watches people shove wads of yellow ghost money into an urn, as well as paper cars and houses, which Jing-wei told her give the dead transportation and housing in the afterlife. Paige doesn't actually know how close she'd come to dying, and she hasn't thought much about it. But here, amid the belief that souls are lost and lonely, that they drift through an eternal purgatory, appeased with food, drink, entertainment, gifts, she can't help but wonder where she might have ended up.

Outside the temple, hogs are being prepared for roasting. Slit open through the belly, eyes and snouts bruised and black, they're spread across red metal racks, their entrails hanging off center rails. The wafting scent of incense masks the stench of blood and death.

She follows the procession until it reaches the water. There the parade marchers take the lanterns off their poles and set them afloat. The lanterns bob gently as they drift out to sea, some extinguished by waves or by the splash of other lanterns swimming past. Paige sees shapes of light hovering above the water—probably the mist in the air, or the effects of Abbey's hash, or of the tears that suddenly rise in her eyes—but she stands still and watches for a long time, until the lights and voices fade away.

Outside, dark clouds billow overhead like puffed steel, and large raindrops begin to fall, hitting the glass of the window. Sitting in the McDonald's, waiting for Jing-wei, Paige shivers. Even during Taipei's bone-chilling winter, the restaurants remain air-conditioned. For the past several months, she has felt as if she would never warm up. Nothing helps—not the lightning pace of running around after her young students, not the heat generated under the sheets of Gabe's bed.

What she does look forward to are her lessons with Jing-wei. They meet twice a week and spend less time on Chinese and more time on each other. Paige doesn't know whether it's Jing-wei's guileless eyes, or the language barrier, or the fact that she is thousands of miles from everything she's ever known—but she has found herself telling Jing-wei things she's never told anyone. Her father's death when she was four; her mother's alcoholic haze. The revolving door of men—the first one, her mother's boyfriend, the one who, in return for her silence, gave her enough money to cover her first semester of college; and the last one, her boss, the one who, predictably, finally chose his wife. She has begun to say it all out loud, for the first time.

At last she sees Jing-wei hurry to the door.

"*Dui bu chi*," Jing-wei apologizes, shrugging off her raincoat and sliding into the plastic seat across from her. "Sorry I'm late. I am so busy today."

"Is everything okay?" Paige asks. The circles under Jing-wei's eyes, which Paige noticed the last time they met, have deepened, and she looks paler than usual.

"Oh yes," Jing-wei says. "*Ni hen mang ma?*" she adds quickly, asking if Paige is busy.

"*Bu mang*," she answers, feeling hopelessly American. "*Shenme ni shi mang?*" She knows, even as the sloppily translated words stumble from her mouth, that it is a terrible attempt at asking Jing-wei why she is so busy.

But her clumsy phrasing is worth it; it draws an unexpected smile to Jing-wei's lips. "Forget English," she says. "If you think in English, it is more hard to understand. You have to think in Chinese. You have to start over."

She opens the textbook, though clearly her mind is elsewhere. "I have date tonight," she confesses. "It is difficult, sometimes, to hide." She pauses. "Can I ask favor?"

"Of course."

"Can I tell my parents I am with you?" Jing-wei asks. "They know all my friends, so it is not safe to say I am with them."

"You can tell them anything you want."

"*Xie xie.* Thank you."

Paige watches Jing-wei's tense face as she flips through her book; she hasn't prepared anything to teach. "Are you sure you're okay?" Paige asks again.

Jing-wei nods, then says, "Soon it will be the Year of the Goat, you know."

"What does that mean?"

"There will be disharmony," she says. "Some trouble from Horse Year will continue."

"What kind of trouble?"

"Goat is very strong animal," Jing-wei says. "Goats stand on steep mountains without falling down. They are sturdy. They survive. At the end is peace. But not in the beginning."

"What will happen at the beginning?"

"I will tell you more when we meet again," she says abruptly. "Let's study travel words."

Paige doesn't know how far to push, so she lowers her eyes to the book. She steals a glance at Jing-wei and sees that her jaw is clenched, as if she is holding back tears. She seems to need all her energy to focus on the moment. When their time is up, she apologizes again. "I must hurry," she says.

"Okay," Paige says. "See you next time, then."

Jing-wei nods. Paige sits in the booth with their two empty cups and watches Jing-wei exit the glass doors and disappear.

Before their next meeting, Paige looks in the mirror, noticing for the first time that her hair has grown far past her shoulders. It has been nearly a year since she's had a haircut. She stops at a neighborhood salon, where she leans back in the chair as the stylist washes her hair, gently massaging her shoulders before beginning the cut. She grows so relaxed that she pays little attention until the stylist steps back to admire the result. Paige glances in the mirror to see that her hair has been cut to her chin. She hardly recognizes herself.

She jumps up. "It's too short," she says. She can't think of the words in Chinese, then realizes that it doesn't matter.

The stylist gently pushes her back down and lifts the scissors again. "No, no," Paige says, adding, "*Bu yao, xie xie.*" She pays quickly and leaves the salon.

Outside, she shivers, her hair still wet. The sky is dark, and an icy rain begins to fall in large, persistent drops. As she hurries toward the McDonald's to meet Jing-wei, a stream of blood-red liquid splatters the top of her shoe. She looks up into the face of a grinning, crimson-toothed man chewing betel nut. He stares at her as she scurries past.

At McDonald's, she huddles over a steaming cup of coffee. Two cups later, Jing-wei still hasn't arrived. Paige tries calling from the pay phone in the back, but there's no one home. She waits through one more cup of coffee, then tries again. This time, a man answers, but he speaks no English, and he doesn't understand her shaky Chinese. She finally has to hang up.

At home, she changes out of her wet clothes before joining Abbey in the living room.

"Don't get your knickers in a twist," Abbey tells her. "I'm sure she's fine."

"She's never missed an appointment," Paige says.

Abbey leans forward and picks up the hash pipe from the coffee table. "Try ringing her once more," she suggests. "Then we'll fire this up. Take your mind off Jing-wei for a while."

Paige dials Jing-wei's number. "*Wei?*" asks a voice, the same one she heard earlier.

"Hello, yes," she says. "I'm calling for Jing-wei." A pause. "*Jing-wei zai ma?*"

"*Bu zai,*" says the man, and continues speaking in Chinese. Paige turns to Abbey. "I can't understand him. Can you help?"

Abbey rises and takes the phone. "*Jing-wei zai bu zai?*" she says. Paige watches her closely, trying to decipher bits of the conversation: *a friend of Jing-wei's . . . where is she? . . .* Then she hears a sharp intake of breath. Abbey turns away, and as Paige strains to hear she sees that Abbey is faltering. Then she hangs up and turns around.

Caught in the thick embrace of Bangkok's unrelenting heat, they duck into a taxi, which twenty minutes later deposits them on a crowded street. Gabe takes Paige's hand and threads them both through the backpackers and street vendors who cram the sidewalks. Down the street, they check into a drab guesthouse.

"It's not the Ritz," Gabe says, "but it's just for tonight. Tomorrow we'll go south, to the beach."

Paige nods. She agreed to come away with Gabe when the school closed for Chinese New Year, not because she really wanted to but because she couldn't stay in Taipei, now that Jing-wei was gone.

That night, even before Abbey told her what had happened, Paige needed no translation. A few days later, with the beginning of Chinese New Year, firecrackers began exploding in the streets, thundering among the buildings, echoing the shock reverberating in Paige's mind. She found herself unable to think straight, unable to think at all, and she soon came to dread the cracking of the explosives and the thin white trails of smoke rising ghostlike in Taipei's misty streets.

Gabe promised warmth and solitude, and she had nothing else to do, nowhere else to go. Now she follows him from the room back to Khao San Road, where the last rays of sun illuminate the jewelry and clothing stalls. She looks down at her bare arms, turning her wrists upward. The scars are now fading from purple to pink, not as badly swollen but still raised. In Taipei, she's been careful to keep them covered, but suddenly she doesn't care who notices.

A thick black curtain hides a large, dark room with a U-shaped bar in the center. Inside, the voices of the Rolling Stones fill the air; girls in bikinis, some topless, dance slowly on an elevated stage in the center of the bar. The bar is crowded with Westerners: men in groups, men with Thai girls.

"What are we doing here?" Paige says.

"I just thought we'd have a drink," Gabe says, "and check out Bangkok's infamous nightlife. Is it too much?"

She shrugs. She knows he's trying. He hands her a beer, and she looks at him over the top of the bottle, his hair curling at the ends from the humid air, his nose peeling from having walked through Bangkok in the heat of midday. They'd had a silent dinner in a noisy backpackers' café, followed by a long ride through the canals. All day, he has snuck worried glances her way, and she's tried to ignore them.

She turns away from his gaze yet again and looks up at the dancers. The girls' movements are slow and bored, their small breasts barely rising above their rib cages, their skin smooth and flawless. A girl with a Band-Aid on her leg leans down to talk to a short, red-faced American. Paige can't hear what they're saying, but eventually the girl climbs down from the stage, the man's arm snaking around her shoulders. An image comes to Paige's mind: Jing-wei and her boyfriend, the nameless, faceless American. She wonders if her parents ever found out who he was, or if the boyfriend ever found out what really happened.

She herself almost hadn't found out. Jing-wei's father had told Abbey that Jing-wei had died in an accident. Then one day, just before leaving for Bangkok, Paige returned from work to find a small box on the table. *Jing-wei's sister stopped by,* Abbey told her. *She found our address in Jing-wei's things. The box had your name on it.*

Paige picked it up and turned it over in her hands, but she didn't open it.

There's something else about Jing-wei, Abbey said, hesitantly. *Her sister said it wasn't an accident. She hanged herself.*

Paige looked up.

She said Jing-wei was pregnant, failing her classes, and she didn't want to shame her family. Her parents have to save face, so they're calling it an accident.

In the bar, Paige watches the dancer smile at the American before they walk away together, the girl's long black hair swinging against his arm, his brown hair combed down against his sunburned neck. Suddenly, Paige feels sick. She flattens her palms against the bar to steady herself.

"Paige?" Gabe's face is close to hers. His mossy green eyes look dark, unreadable. "You okay?"

She doesn't answer. She stands up and rushes past the curtain, outside into the crowded alley. He's right behind her. "Let's get out of here," she says.

"What is it?" he asks.

"I want to go home," she says, and he thinks she means back to the guesthouse.

In their room, he tries to apologize, but she moves to the far side of the bed. "Just tell me what happened back there," he says, and she rolls over.

She feels Gabe lie down gingerly next to her in the bed, and it's a long time before she hears his breathing deepen. When she's sure he's asleep, she gets up and packs what little she's taken out of her bag. She doesn't know where she's going, but she zips it up and leaves it by the door. Then she checks the bathroom to see if she has left anything there.

Fumbling for the light switch, she knocks a glass into the porcelain sink. It shatters.

She peeks into the room to see if the sound awakened Gabe, but it was masked by the noises from the street outside their window. She turns back to the broken glass. She picks up a shard the size of a coin. Instead of dropping it into the wastebasket next to the sink, she finds herself holding it tightly between her thumb and forefinger and stretching her other arm in front of her.

She looks past the pinkish scars on her wrists and focuses instead on the pale flesh inside her forearms, smooth and untouched. Vertical cuts, if they followed the thin blue lines of her veins, wouldn't clot as easily as her previous wounds. This much she now knows.

She draws the glass up one arm, lightly, trailing a scratch from her wrist to her elbow. Then she does it again, harder this time, carving a deeper line that draws blood. Tiny droplets bead up on her skin like sweat. She has only one clear thought: *It's got to work this time. If I do it, I've got to do it right.*

She hadn't let herself think the first time; she hadn't planned to do it. It had been a blind reaction, a desperate wish.

But now she knows differently. Vertical cuts. Lock the door.

She feels a sudden sharp pain and looks down at her hand. The fingers clutching the fragment of glass are wet with blood; the glass had slipped, slicing her thumb. Without thinking, she drops the shard and wraps tissues around the cut.

Then she glances up into the bathroom mirror, catching sight of her face: thin, pale, trailed with tears. She sees new wrinkles around her eyes, creases around her mouth. She leans closer, wondering what she might look like in another year, in ten years, in twenty. The thought of getting that far makes her weary.

As she presses the tissues to her thumb, she finds herself savoring the sting of the cut, the throb of her pulse under the thin folds of cotton. Before, she'd felt nothing.

She hears a knock at the door. "Paige?" Gabe's voice is muffled. "Are you okay?"

She takes a deep breath. "I'm fine," she says. "Be right out."

In the morning, before Gabe wakes up, Paige picks up Jing-wei's box. She holds it for a few moments, afraid to open it, afraid that when she does, Jing-wei might disappear completely, along with everything Paige had shared with her. Suddenly, she doesn't know what she would do without her own history to anchor her, even as she tries to escape it.

She hears Gabe stirring, and she stuffs the box back into her knapsack and dons a long-sleeved T-shirt. When Gabe asks her about the glass in the bathroom, she tells him she knocked it over in the dark. She shows him her thumb, and he lets it go.

They don't talk on the bus ride to Krabi, or on the boat to the island. On the beach, when Gabe goes for a swim, Paige takes out Jing-wei's box again, staring at it for a long time before she opens it.

Inside, nestled into a puff of cotton, lies a pendant made of jade and yellow gold. The cloudy green gemstone is thin and round, with a gold Chinese character squeezed into the middle. An ornate leafy gold pattern grasps the top of the piece, with a hook for a necklace or chain.

She puts a hand to her bare neck, turning over the pendant in her other hand. She looks up to see Gabe emerging from the water, and she shows it to him. "Do you know what the character means?"

Gabe squints at it. "I can't read it. But jade is supposed to bring good luck and long life. The Chinese call it the Stone of Heaven."

Paige folds her hand over it.

"Healers believe jade helps those who have suffered or who are grieving," Gabe says.

Paige leans back on her towel and closes her eyes. When she opens them again, the sun has shifted, and she is hot and sweaty, covered with clothing. She sits up and pulls it all off.

"You were getting sunburned," Gabe says. She looks down at her legs, pink and freckled, then touches her cheeks.

"I covered you up and put sunscreen on your face," he says. "You slept right through it."

"Thanks," she says.

She leaves him and dives into the sea, the calm water soothing. She turns onto her back and floats, and as she drifts on the gentle waves of the bay, she feels, strangely, the way she thought she would feel when she cut her wrists—an ineffable weightlessness, as if she is free, at last, of everything: work, family, men, loneliness, regret, her very self. She floats as if she has become a part of the ocean, mingling with its salty tide.

She hears a splash and looks up to see Gabe nearby. When he swims over, she puts her arms around his neck.

"I wanted—" he begins.

"Shhh." She leans back, dipping her head into the water, then straightening up to look at him. The sun is freckling his skin, his eyes a

luminous green. Water drips from his eyelashes and from the wet strands
of his hair. She kisses him and, forgetting the others on the beach,
reaches down to the elastic of his swim trunks. Seized by a sudden,
overwhelming desire, she feels as if, right then, by taking his body into
hers she can stay forever in the present, in the world of the physical and
all its sensations, and everything else will disappear.

He whispers something that she doesn't hear and starts swimming
away. She swims alongside him, to the end of the beach where the cliffs
meet the water. He leads her to a cave. Inside, it's dark and damp, and
when her eyes adjust she turns back toward the entrance, seeing nothing but the white glow of afternoon. Under her, the sand is cool and
wet, a salve against her sunburned shoulders.

Back in Taipei, the firecrackers are nearly as constant as before the
New Year. Paige winces as a group of kids sets off a brick in the alley
behind the jewelry shop. She has to take a deep breath before she can
speak.

The owner is a wizened man with reddish teeth stained by betel nut.
He speaks broken English, and Paige uses gestures and her limited Chinese vocabulary to show him what she wants. After being presented
with various gold chains and prices scrawled on the back of a newspa-
per in the man's wobbly script, she chooses one.

Then she shows him the pendant. "Do you know what this means?"
She struggles to find the words in Chinese, pointing to the character.
"*Zhe shi shenme?*"

He understands. "Ah, yes," he says. "'Lucky.'" He nods and points to
the character. "It mean 'good fortune.'"

Paige walks toward the night market to meet Gabe. She doesn't see
him near the alley, so she waits, watching the couples and families go
past.

She thinks of a story Jing-wei once told her—she called it *fu shui nan
shou*. Jing-wei said in English it meant "spilled water can't be recovered,"

and it was about a peasant whose wife left him because he was poor. He later became a high-ranking official, Jing-wei said, and then his wife wanted him back. So he threw water on the ground, and he told his wife to pick it up. Of course, she couldn't—it had turned to mud. And he told her, "See? It's impossible to undo what you've done."

It is like me, with my family, Jing-wei had said, worry furrowing her brow. *I can never undo my lies.*

Of course you can, Paige had said. *It's never too late.* Her words had surprised her even as she said them. Now she wants to believe them.

Gabe hasn't shown up, and when Paige remembers the new teacher at the school, it occurs to her that perhaps he isn't coming. She waits a few more minutes, then walks into the market alone, looking at the vendors, the goods, the shoppers. What had at one time seemed strange and jarring, even magical, has grown familiar: the hot white lights; the tones of the language; the pungent scent of foods once exotic, now commonplace. In the warm and dewy air, the chill of spring clings to a breeze that washes over her, and she feels Jing-wei's pendant rest in the hollow of her neck, the jade cool against her throat.

REST OF WORLD

San Francisco

DAY ONE

The red message light on the phone is blinking, and I pick up the receiver. "This is the concierge, calling for Joyce," says a smooth male voice, "to confirm your dinner reservation at Aqua for seven-thirty, party of two. If you have any questions, feel free to call us at extension 48."

I hang up, wishing my name were Joyce. I draw a bath, for one.

I'm on the first leg of a three-city business trip on which I need to lay off two more data analysts and tell those remaining how the company's reorganization will change their jobs. Our new owners, who made an appearance in New York as part of the takeover two months ago before returning to their golf games in Florida, had informed us of their strategy during a phone conference last week. My colleagues tell me we should feel lucky that, as senior management, we haven't been reorganized out of *our* jobs. Not yet, anyway.

I bought two books before I left—*Tough Decisions: How a Good Manager Handles Being the Bad Guy* and *Broken Trust: Recovering from Infidelity*. Not long before I learned about the reorganization, my husband had confessed that he was cheating on me. Unlike my bosses, at least Kyle conveyed his news in person, although he didn't look me in the eye. I couldn't fathom how I would restructure either my department or my marriage. In my desperation, I could only buy books.

I step into the water, easing down against the clammy ceramic of the bathtub. But instead of relaxing, I'm overwhelmed by a sense that I'm disappearing, melting into the water—that if I open the plug under my feet, I might drain away and be gone. I find myself wondering whether Joyce ever got her message. I picture showing up in her place at Aqua, surprising her date. He would look up, bemused, then smile and offer me a chair. Later, he would take me back to his penthouse and make love to me.

The fantasy comes easily because this was essentially how I met Kyle. Six years ago, after finishing an early dinner with a friend, I stopped for coffee at a crowded café. Kyle's blind date hadn't shown, and he offered me the seat he'd been saving. We talked half the night and kissed on a subway platform in Brooklyn. We married two years later. Now he's sleeping with our neighbor, a tall French woman named Margot, and I'm sleeping alone, three thousand miles away.

DAY TWO

Kyle hasn't called. Before I left New York, I emailed him my itinerary, and it had occurred to me when I hit "Send" that our communication had been primarily electronic long before we separated. Between work and a long-distance marriage, my world had become largely virtual, ephemeral, my existence reduced to the click of a keyboard.

I'm not sure why I hope Kyle will call, except that I long for the familiarity of his voice. It reminds me that I'm still anchored to the world, a feeling I tend to lose when I travel, a feeling I've lost almost completely since losing him. I'm away six months out of a year, and when I'm home, I'm usually either gearing up for another trip or coming down from one.

Broken Trust tells me it's not my fault that my husband cheated; it happened because of *his* weaknesses. The author's bold convictions, punctuated with exclamation points, dare me to believe them, but I know better. Early in our marriage, when I was away, I'd call Kyle every night before going to sleep, no matter how late the hour, and he never minded being woken up. Now I'll forgo having dinner with him so that I can rest before a big trip, and he no longer waits up for me when I'm due home. It's almost hard to remember that we once lost sleep for each other, that new love knows no such thing as weariness or inconvenience. We used to follow nearly every trip with a romantic weekend together, to make up for lost time. But slowly we allowed that time to remain lost.

I shower and put on a navy pantsuit. This won't be the hardest day—no one in the San Francisco office will be fired—but they'll surely balk at the higher numbers we've set for Q3 and Q4. It took me twelve years, five at this company, to earn a vice presidency, a position I think about often these days. I've spent my career at telecommunications research firms arguing about price dynamics, deconstructing such trends as global roaming. I work hard to predict emerging markets—and yet I can't figure out how a marriage works. I don't have the tools to forecast where Kyle and I will be in a year, or even a month. I certainly did not forecast where we'd be right now.

He told me about his affair on a weeknight. When I asked whether he was in love with her, he said he didn't know. I moved out immediately, thinking I never wanted to see him again, and rented a furnished studio in midtown. It had not occurred to me at the time to kick him out—the author of *Broken Trust* would be gravely disappointed in me—but I suppose I was just so used to being the one leaving that it came naturally. After all, my bags are perpetually packed.

Now I wish I hadn't left. Night after night, I've sat alone on the convertible sofa, listening to the drone of the refrigerator and the traffic sparring below and wondering whether Kyle felt this way when I traveled. My apartment is so void of promise that entering empty hotel rooms now feels like coming home.

DAY THREE

I wake slightly hungover. Paul, our senior analyst in San Francisco, met me in the hotel bar last night before our client dinner. We've worked together for six years. I received a courtesy invitation to his wedding in Savannah, and I drank with him three years later in Singapore after his wife filed for divorce. When I told him that Kyle and I had separated, he ordered me a double and kept saying, *If you ever want to talk* . . . But I don't. I fear that his advice would be like that of a fortune-teller whose prophecy I don't want to hear.

Paul is thirty-eight, with the receding hair and expanding paunch of someone you'd expect to see at a backyard barbecue filled with children. Now he's dating, or trying to. As we sat at the bar, I watched his eyes drift toward a woman who had entered alone, watched his hope rise and fade, and in that moment I thought, *I've got to make it work with Kyle*. Then I ordered another drink.

As I pop aspirin, I remember that trip to Singapore, how one day I'd wandered into an electronics store, mostly to escape the heat, and stood in front of a wall of plasma TV screens, watching one of the local programs. I hadn't noticed that a woman was standing next to me until a commercial came on. The ad showed a sad little boy asking his parents when they were going to give him a little brother—one of the government's family-friendly promotions that were everywhere back then. The woman asked me whether I had any children, and I said no. She told me that she thought I would make an excellent mother because I looked very smart and had a good, sturdy figure.

I think about this now, as I pack for my next flight. Kyle and I had talked about children during the first couple years we were married, but we decided to wait until things settled down. Until I settled down. And so it never happened.

Before going downstairs, I text Kyle, reminding him that my cell phone coverage is spotty once I leave the country and giving him the phone numbers of my next two hotels. A part of me whispers, *Just call him.* But I'm afraid. That he won't be home at ten o'clock on a weekend morning. That Margot will answer. That he'll pick up the phone and ask, "Who is this?"

Before leaving, I scan the room for anything I might have missed. I walk through the bathroom, open dresser drawers and the closet. For the first time, the ritual saddens me—the fact that I leave nothing behind. Even Joyce left a vestige of her time here. After one last look around the empty room, I close the door behind me.

Taipei

DAY ONE

When I enter my room, bleary-eyed from the flight, the bellhop says something to me in Chinese, too rapidly for me to understand. I have to ask him, in English, whether he speaks English—one of my ugly American flaws. I had studied French and a little Spanish in school—

romance languages, ironically—but years later, as I attempted to learn Chinese and Japanese, it seemed too late to retrain my own mind.

I pick up the phone and find a saved message—a reminder, I suppose, that our recently trimmed budget means staying in hotels that don't routinely delete leftover voice mail. Yet I'm grateful for something to listen to: a message for a man named Stan, comprising detailed directions to a meeting that apparently took place yesterday.

I look at the files of the two employees who will be let go and try to rehearse how I'll break the news to them. I think about how Kyle broke the news to me. We sat through an entire dinner at home, as if everything were normal; we drank half a bottle of wine. He refilled my glass and said, "I'm sorry." Then he told me.

It's similar with layoffs: we try to cushion the blow by easing into it; we apologize first. I flip through my two books until they fuse in my mind. *Tough Decisions* points out that layoffs and restructuring are part of the natural cycle of a business. I can only hope that is also true of a marriage, that our situation is a necessary shake-up, something that will only strengthen us in the end.

DAY TWO

At 9:40 local time, I fire a man who supports his wife and three-year-old daughter. At 10:20, I fire a woman who relocated to Taipei six months ago for the job.

We're always hearing about how the world is shrinking, becoming a "global village," but to me it is steadily growing more vast, more impenetrable. I can see in the eyes of these two employees that the world is now too big for them. Like me, they're frozen with the fear of having to take their next step. Choices are a luxury they don't want.

At 11:15, I throw up in the ladies' room.

The fact that our employees always seem to know what's coming doesn't make this easier. I can see it in their faces, in their clenched hands, as they wait for me to tell them they're losing their jobs. For them, the signs are all too obvious: executives flying in from the head office, email attachments warning of dismal earnings reports, the language of downsizing, in which we are all fluent.

I spend the afternoon in meetings with our diminished staff. Everything now seems like a zero-sum game; two people lose their jobs, and
the sales team gains a budget. My job takes me away from Kyle, and a
French woman takes Kyle away from me. Business and love operate on
the same principles of reciprocity, of gains and losses.

Our firm's research spans Asia, Latin America, and Europe. We use
the term *rest of world* to categorize markets that are just emerging or
are still very small—markets that we don't yet study independently. For
some companies, the term is a cop-out. They study three or four re-
gions and use *rest of world* to describe the dozens of countries they ne-
glect to consider. I think about this later, as I return to my room after
another liquor-soaked client dinner. The focal point of my life has always been my career—what's left has been relegated to *rest of marriage,
rest of life.*

I get into bed and listen to Stan's message again. I turn my head one
way, then the other, wondering which side of the bed Stan slept on,
then shift onto my belly and stretch my arms and legs as far as they will
reach. I try to fill Stan's former space, in some strange attempt to feel
that I'm not quite sleeping alone.

DAY THREE

Outside, the air and sky are shadows of one another, a cold, sodden
gray that seeps inexorably into my mood. I see the spatter of rain on the
window and feel like burrowing deeper into the blankets, hibernating
until I can get a firmer grasp on everything that seems to be slipping
through my fingers. But meetings await.

After lunch, I'm free until my flight that evening—always a temporary freedom, nothing more than *rest of time.* The rain has stopped, and
I pack and leave my bags with the concierge. I spend a couple of hours
in a teahouse with my books, searching for answers I'm not finding.

On my way back to the hotel, I wander through a street market,
where I buy a plate of dumplings from a vendor and settle down at a
nearby table. After trying without success to eat them with slippery
plastic chopsticks, I use my fingers. The flavor lingers on my hands.

I sit for a while at the fold-out table that constitutes the dining area.
The chairs are flimsy, portable, like everything else—the food carts, the

makeshift restaurants that surround them, the thin-legged tables laden with clothing and imitation jewelry. Every day, these vendors unpack their wares, cook their meals, then pack up and go away, the essence of their livelihoods moveable and temporary. I search their faces for signs of weariness or resignation, for signs of loneliness, but as they shout across the alleyway and joke with one another, I detect only the underlying glow of muted happiness.

Tokyo

DAY ONE

The shades in my tiny, spartan hotel room are open to the fading light of the disappearing sun, to the pinkish glow of the sunset on Mount Fuji. I find a new message on the voice mail. I don't retrieve it right away, not sure I'm ready to hear what Kyle has to say. I use the bathroom, wash my face and hands. Then I pick up the phone.

The message is not for me but for someone called Barb; a man named Gregory leaves the name of a restaurant where they're supposed to meet later. I sigh and look around the empty room. One missed call, and three people will eat alone tonight.

I listen to the message again. I wonder who Gregory is and what will happen if Barb doesn't show up. I think about the last time I sat down to a dinner that wasn't a business meeting and realize it was the night Kyle told me about his affair.

Looking at the bedside alarm clock, I make a decision. I shower off my flight from Taipei and slather on the exotic sandalwood lotion in the hotel bathroom. I've brought nothing but business suits, so I hurry down to the gift shop, where I buy an overpriced green silk blouse and a pair of jade earrings. I can't remember the last time I wore anything other than black, beige, or navy.

When I tell the restaurant's hostess that my name is Barb, she leads me to a table where a man sits alone. Gregory looks at me suspiciously, and I explain that he dialed the wrong room, that because he hadn't left a number, I had no other way of letting him know. His gaze softens, and he politely invites me to join him. Of course, I haven't given him much choice.

We introduce ourselves and chat for a few moments. He's in sales, he tells me. Barb, it turns out, is a colleague; if there's more between them, he doesn't say. Then he asks why I came all the way to the restaurant just to tell him that he'd misdialed.

I don't have a good answer for him, and the term *global roaming*, ubiquitous in my industry, suddenly takes on a new meaning: I am halfway across the world with a salesman from New Jersey, while my husband is in New York with a French fashion editor. But this variation on the term is something I can't yet define.

"Are you married?" I ask him instead, and in response he shows me a photograph of his kids: a four-year-old girl and a two-year-old boy. I see his wedding ring as he reaches across the table to hand me the photo, but he doesn't talk about his wife. He doesn't ask whether I'm married.

After dinner, he insists on picking up the tab, and I catch the flash of a familiar silver-gray: a corporate AmEx card. Outside, a light mist has begun to fall, and he looks up the street for a taxi. Most of the cabs already have passengers. He takes off his coat and puts it across my shoulders, then invites me back to his hotel for a drink.

In the awkward space of my hesitation, he turns back to the road, resuming his search for a taxi. I'm flattered, and perhaps a bit grateful, that despite my "sturdy" figure and the plum-colored circles under my eyes, I can still capture a man's interest, if not my own husband's. But while *Broken Trust* might urge readers to "get on with your life" and "live like the passionate person that you are," I'm thinking now of *Tough Decisions*. Any solution that seems too easy, its author counsels, nearly always is.

I tell Gregory that I have an early meeting and have to get back. The rain is picking up again, and he seems relieved when he finally hails a cab. I hand over his jacket as he gives the driver the name of my hotel, and the taxi pulls away. After only a few moments, the inside of the cab begins to feel suffocating, and I ask the driver to stop and let me out. I walk the rest of the way, the rain soaking through my new silk blouse, each drop like the touch of soft fingers on the fabric.

DAY TWO

I spend the next day in our Tokyo office. Between meetings, I try to
check my cell phone for voice mail before remembering that it doesn't
work on the local networks. I return to the hotel after six o'clock to
find two messages, one from Gregory, who wonders whether I'm free
this evening, and the other from Kyle, who must have called from his
cell phone. What he says is hard to hear but easy to decipher: *make some
decisions . . . called a lawyer . . . talk when we get home . . .*

Instead of returning the calls, I turn off my cell phone and head back
to the street. I find a noodle shop a few blocks away. Inside, I savor the
way the little room fills my senses—the heat emanating from the kitch-
en, the steam lining the inside of the windows, the scent of the broth,
the sting of it on my tongue—all the things I've shut out over the years,
like the little dent in Kyle's chin, the taste of his lips after a long weekend run.

Back in my room, before going to bed, I unplug the phone.

DAY THREE

My business done, my bags nearly packed, I check email in the hotel
room to pass the time before my flight back to New York. I receive a
memo from my division head, telling me that our new owners are flying
in next week for another series of meetings. It is just vague enough to
be alarming. The latest financials are attached. Words swim, surreal, on
my computer screen: *continued reorganization . . . further adjustments . . .
best interests of the company.*

I close my laptop and lay my head down on top of it, the heat of the
battery warming my face. I lose track of time, and when I hear a knock
on the door, I remember having called the bellhop earlier to pick up
my bags.

I let him in, tossing the rest of my clothes into my suitcase, papers
into my briefcase. I start to check the room, as usual, to make sure I
haven't forgotten anything. Then I stop myself.

I leave the unanswered messages from Kyle and Gregory on the hotel's voice mail. I leave the two books stacked on the coffee table. The
green silk blouse, stained dark from the rain, hangs limply in the closet.

DAY FOUR

Yesterday I missed my flight, only the third time during all my years of travel. I've always taken pride in accuracy, in good timing, in precision. The other two missed flights were due to unavoidable traffic delays; this one I missed because I asked the taxi driver to take me to the train station instead of the airport. Now, from my seat inside the tube of the *shinkansen* bullet train, the landscape of southern Japan blurs past.

I spent last night in Kyoto but wanted to continue on, to get as far as possible from the point where I began. I've been to Japan eleven times and have never left Tokyo, have never traveled outside the boundaries of layovers and deadlines.

My next stop is Hiroshima. I bought an English-language travel book in the train station this morning, and I read that after the mass devastation of the atomic bomb, despite having lost nearly half its population in the blast, the city had its public transportation up and running again within weeks. All at once, people mourned and moved on. Then they dedicated the site to peace.

For the first time, I'm a tourist, and when I visit the Hiroshima Peace Memorial, I see the burned-out dome that has been preserved for over half a century, bricks still lying next to broken walls, bits of steel peeling away from the building. And signs of life: new grass growing amid the wreckage, cats peeking out from glassless windows.

After today, I will continue south. Eventually I'll be able to go no further; I'll reach end of country, end of road. And then, I suppose, I'll turn around.

BEYOND THE KOPJES

The lodge is in the middle of the Serengeti and built like an African village, with small, round buildings and thatched roofs. As the Land Cruiser bounces along the rock-strewn road, Dana notices two Cape buffalo lying nearby, not far from a cluster of bungalows. They're the size of bulls, with curved horns extending from the tops of their heads into sharp, graceful points. They lie dark and dusty in the tall grass, nostrils flaring as the vehicle approaches.

The Cape buffalo, their guide, Bakari, had told them in Ngorongoro, *are among the most dangerous and unpredictable animals in Tanzania.*

They look harmless to me, Bryan had said. *Like cows.*

This is why they are dangerous, Bakari said. *People underestimate them. They may be herbivores, but they will attack anything if they feel threatened.*

Now, as they pass, Dana's mind flashes to a dusky parking lot, a bloodied nose. She shakes off the memory, leans forward, and calls to Bakari, "Those buffalo are a little close to the lodge, aren't they?"

"It's okay," Bakari says. "They're old, and vulnerable to the lions. And they know the lions don't like to come near the lodge. So they are safe here."

"Yes, but are we?" Dana asks. She's five-two, and she now knows that she can fight off a man twice her size, but the buffalo make her nervous.

Bakari smiles as they reach the lodge's entrance. Dana waits outside as Bryan follows him and the others into the reception area. The group had just landed at the game reserve's gravel airstrip, their last stop on a twelve-day safari, and though it is late afternoon, a heavy, dry heat still clutches the air.

Bryan fumbles with the key in the old-fashioned lock. Their bungalow is near the lodge's entrance, where the sculpted landscaping gives way to the wild plains of the reserve. Dana peers through the trees, knowing the buffalo are somewhere just beyond.

Inside, Dana lies down on the bed, staring at the folds of mosquito netting gathered at the canopy above. She feels the bed sink with Bryan's weight.

"Why don't you take a quick nap," he suggests.

"I'm all right." It's been two years since she's been able to sleep at will, to turn everything off and let herself rest. Two years, and she still keeps pills on hand: the prescriptions for Xanax that Bryan writes for her, the Tylenol with codeine that her sister gets over the counter in Vancouver. She drinks, too, a couple glasses of wine at dinner, another one or two before bed. And still the night stretches out before her, a long, flat, endless plain of sleeplessness, its topography mapped by the feel of hands on her neck, hair ripping from her scalp. She can never remember the moment at which her eyes finally close. She no longer sinks gently into sleep; it's more as if she simply stops being awake.

Bryan stretches out next to her. "Want to take a shower?" he says, his fingers outlining her neck, her collarbone.

"You go ahead."

She turns to watch him cross the room before letting her eyes settle into a crack on the wall. After showering, Bryan goes to check out the gift shop before dinner. She meets him later, in the dining room.

The rest of their group is already there: Dusty, a software developer from California, and Patrick and Jill, an older couple, probably in their fifties, from Rhode Island. Bakari sits at the head, a father figure. He is a native Tanzanian, from the Iraqw tribe, and, with his stocky build and round, uncreased face, at sixty he still looks forty. "Tomorrow will be a full day," he says. "We will meet for breakfast at six so we can be in the park before it gets too hot."

At the end of their meal, Bakari excuses himself to speak to their driver. Dana and Bryan join the others in the lounge, where glasses of whiskey and Kilimanjaro Beer soon fill the small tables in front of them.

As Jill and Patrick engage Bryan in a conversation about pharmaceuticals, Dana looks up to find Dusty watching her. It's not the first time, and she isn't sure why. He looks to be in his early thirties and lives in Santa Cruz, his suntan and fair hair making her suddenly feel old and pale. Tonight, in the dim lights of the lounge, his brown eyes look velvety and dark.

"So what's your latest article about?" he asks.

"Um, it was just a piece for a fitness magazine," she says. She doesn't add that it was a short column about the nutritional value of the potato, that it required no real reporting and virtually no actual writing. She calls herself a freelance writer to mask the fact that she hasn't really worked for nearly four years. She and Bryan had married young, and after he finished medical school and his career was well under way, she decided she wanted a change, so she'd enrolled in a journalism program. And her life had transformed, though not in any of the ways she'd expected.

You don't have to work until you're ready, Bryan always tells her. He travels quite often—medical conferences, mostly—and for the past couple of years, she has agreed with him, needing the freedom to join him so she doesn't have to stay alone in the city.

Before Dusty can ask her which magazine, she stands. "Be right back."

She heads toward the bar before he can respond. She orders another chardonnay and another whiskey for Bryan, but after she signs the bill, she remains standing, her back to the room, and sips the wine. When she finishes her glass, she orders another and returns to the group. Dusty is gone.

Later, when she's ready for bed, she watches her reflection in the sliding glass door as she walks toward it to pull the curtains shut. She's smaller than she used to be, her curves shrunken to straight, boyish lines, her face leaner and sharper. The darkness outside is so complete that the door is like a mirror. She cracks it open.

Outside, a small patio gives way to a forest of acacias illuminated by orange spotlights. Past the trees, lights flicker from a boxy, utilitarian building. A dimly lit path winds between their bungalow and the clearing where the Cape buffalo live. She watches the shadows of the trees dapple the wooden planks of the porch, the thin slats of the chairs. She jumps when she feels Bryan's arms around her waist, from behind.

"You always sneak up on me like that," she says.

"I wasn't sneaking," he says. "I just asked you if you were ready for bed."

"I didn't hear you." She slides the door shut, and her face appears in the glass again, next to Bryan's. He tightens his arms around her. "You're safe now," he says.

She fights the urge to pull away.

"I saw you talking to Dusty," he says.

"For two seconds," she says. Moments like these make her wonder whether he knows. She doesn't think he ever found out, but he always seems just shy of suspicious.

"Come on," he says. "Let's go to bed."

In bed, he pulls her close, tucking her into the space between his arm and shoulder. She waits until his breathing deepens before she moves away. Then she lies awaiting sleep, staring up at the ghostlike shroud of the mosquito net, feeling trapped and weighed down, even though it hangs far above her, so sheer and light that it flutters in the ceiling fan's breeze.

Bryan had been the one to rescue her that night, to interrupt what could have been far worse than what she'd already endured. They were living in a brownstone then, a charming walk-up that a month later they would trade for a full-security building with a doorman.

She'd opened the door expecting someone else. But the man who stood there had grabbed her before she could make a sound, clapped a hand over her mouth, and shoved her inside, kicking the door shut.

He dragged her just a few feet, pushed her to the floor, and even as she struggled to free herself she wondered how anyone could be that strong, how anyone could render her that completely helpless. When she heard Bryan's voice, she thought she must have passed out and been dreaming, or that she was already dead—but suddenly she felt the pressure lift from her throat, her chest, and she was coughing and gasping for air, and then flailing at Bryan, not realizing that her attacker had darted past him and out the door, down the back stairwell.

Bryan examined her throat, checked her ribs, and looked for cuts under her torn clothing. He called the police, gave her a sedative, held her until she finally slept. And every time she awoke that night, he too was awake, reassuring her that she was safe.

She no longer opens doors to strangers, and she scans parking lots like a Secret Service agent—but she still finds that sleep, that most vulnerable state, is hard to come by. Bryan encouraged her to take self-defense classes, which helped more than therapy. She knows now that criminals rarely choose their victims randomly, that the perception of vulnerability increases one's odds of becoming a victim, that such simple steps as not opening a door or pausing in the dark will keep you safe 90 percent of the time.

This is what she wished she'd known that night, five simple words: *set, brace, hook, bridge, roll.* The tae kwon do instructors, two second-degree black belts, had drilled the words into them, over and over, reminding them that although they may not have time to think in an emergency, with enough repetition of the words and the corresponding moves, their bodies would remember.

She still runs through the moves in her head sometimes, but when she does, she imagines herself as she had been, on her back, already pinned down by his weight, his hands at her throat. This time, her mind tells her, *set*: and she lifts her arms over her head, bringing them down fast, into the crooks of the man's elbows, collapsing him forward, bringing his face even closer to hers. Her mind continues, *brace*: bringing up her knees, heels to her tailbone, putting her in a position of power. Then the *hook*, trapping his foot with her own, ensuring that he can't get away. Then the classic martial arts moves: *bridge*—lifting him up, throwing him off balance—and *roll*, heaving him to the side, taking back control.

It took a long time to get comfortable with the notion of bringing her enemy closer in order to get away. But the first time she was able to lift a two-hundred-pound man off her hundred-pound frame and toss him aside, she accepted it. She sometimes thinks back to the moment she lashed out at Bryan, just after he'd come to her rescue. Sometimes, in the dark, with his head bent over hers, his weight on her body, he feels less and less like her rescuer.

The female raises her head and gazes irritably at the male, then lifts a paw and swipes at his face. The male grunts and backs away.

"Ouch," Dusty says.

"The worst rejection ever," Patrick says. "In front of all these people, too." Twelve other safari vehicles are lined up on the road, all angling for views.

The female gets to her feet and begins walking toward the road. "During the mating," Bakari says, "the male has to follow the female. Everything is up to her."

"Story of my life," Patrick says.

"Yeah, right," says Jill.

The lions stroll across the road, threatening to disappear into the tall grasses on the other side. The Land Cruiser's driver, a tall, gangly Maasai named Victor, quickly backs up and maneuvers around the other vehicles for a better spot. But the lions, unmoved by the sound of engines and several dozen cameras, settle down only a short distance from the road. They are five yards from Dana's telephoto lens. The female opens her mouth, yawns, and then gazes toward the vehicles with heavy eyelids. Dana sits down and lets her elbows nudge out the window, keeping her eye in the viewfinder. Through the lens, the lions look close enough to touch, every detail sharp: the tufts of fur on their ears, the salt-and-pepper whiskers, the sprinkle of pink across black noses.

Behind her, she hears Jill ask, "The cars don't bother them?"

"This generation of lions has grown up around the vehicles," Bakari says. "They are not afraid, unless they see you standing on two legs. If you want to die right now, open your door and step out."

"They'll attack, just like that?"

"They will not hesitate," Bakari says.

The female rises again, walking about twenty feet away, into the partial shade of an acacia tree. The male follows close behind, pausing behind her before climbing onto her back. This time, she lets him.

"He's biting her neck," Patrick says, watching through binoculars.

"It's called foreplay, honey," Jill says.

Dana stands, but by the time she pops her head out of the open roof, the male is already lying next to the female, and they're both staring off into the distance.

"That's it?" Jill says, then laughs. "Story of *my* life."

"Very funny," Patrick says.

Victor starts the engine and turns around. The dry yellowish grasses stretch as far as Dana can see—forever, unobstructed, no surprises. The thought comforts her until Victor breaks the silence.

"*Duma*," he says, pointing ahead. "Cheetah."

Dana stands up, seeing nothing. Finally, she finds them: two lean, small-headed cats lying in the tall grass, facing in opposite directions. Covering each other.

Dana squints, studying the landscape, wondering how much more lies beyond her scope of vision. Everything in Tanzania seems hidden. At the Maasai kopjes—clusters of egg-shaped rocks the size of three-, four-, and five-story buildings—they search for the creatures that take refuge under the rocks. They drive around twice, finding nothing.

Back on the main road, Dana stands, her head out the top, wind-driven bugs smacking into her skin, clothes, sunglasses. Suddenly the truck hits a hole; she tumbles forward, and then feels herself caught, lifted, everything tilted: the rim of Dusty's hat; his hair against the back of his neck; a bicep, flexed as it holds her weight.

Quickly, she steps away, flustered. Bryan is on his feet, concerned, and she says, irritably, "I'm fine," and waves him back to his seat.

She sits down in the back. When they approach the lodge, she looks for the buffalo, sticking her head out the window when she doesn't see them. Finally, she finds them grazing nearby, nearly hidden among the trees. *We are kopjes for the buffalo,* she thinks, then realizes that she's been holding her breath.

After dinner, the whiskey glasses are refilled again and again, but Bakari doesn't drink. He sips from a glass of water as he tells them about his name. "It is a Kiswahili name," he says, "meaning *one with great promise.* I am an Iraqw, but in my family we all have Kiswahili names. We have one hundred and twenty tribes in Tanzania, but we are united through our national language."

Dana's glass is empty. "Another drink, anyone?"

"The waiter will be back," Bryan says.

"I want to stretch my legs." She walks up to the bar, and a moment later Dusty appears next to her and orders a whiskey. She glances back toward Bryan, who is still listening to Bakari.

She remembers the feel of Dusty's arms around her earlier, the way her instinct had failed her, unlike that time in the parking lot back home. About a month after the attack, she'd been carrying a heavy load of groceries to her car when a man had touched her arm—apparently attempting to offer her help with her bags. In response, she'd spun around, dropping her groceries, and flattened her palm against his nose. It had taken several attorney conferences and a small settlement to avoid litigation, but she didn't regret it for a minute. When Dusty caught her earlier, part of her was relieved that she hadn't had a similar reaction. Another part of her was worried.

"What are you thinking?" he asks her.

Just then, it hits her. "You remind me of someone," she says.

"Who?"

But she can't tell him, so she shakes her head.

"So how long have you and Bryan been married?" he asks.

"About fifteen years," she says. "What about you? Ever get lonely, traveling by yourself?"

"Hope not," he says. "I'm headed to South Africa after this, for another two weeks."

"That's where I wanted to go," she says, "but Bryan wanted Tanzania."

"So ditch him in Arusha and come with me."

She laughs. "Sure."

He looks at her, and she turns her gaze down into her glass. In the pale amber liquid she sees a wavering image of her face. She glances up and sees Bryan approaching.

"Well, it's getting late," Dusty says. "See you tomorrow."

Feeling Bryan's eyes on her, she doesn't watch Dusty leave. Instead she downs her wine.

Back in the room, as she lies in bed, the night is so quiet she can hear Bryan's toothbrush against his teeth, the gentle drift of water from a bottle as he rinses his brush. His flashlight creates a bluish glow around his sunburned face just before he shuts it off.

He struggles with the netting, and when he climbs inside, she pretends to be asleep. After a while, she hears the deep pull of his breathing and finally relaxes. She needs to know that he's there, yet asleep. He has become the kopje whose shade she needs in order to rest—a place where she can be safe, yet alone.

Things had been tense between them for a while before the attack—they'd both known it but hadn't addressed it. In the journalism program, being one of only two students over thirty, she had put the work ahead of the problems in their marriage. And then there was Rick.

Rick was the other older student, an inveterate traveler who'd just returned to what he called "real life," and he was the one she'd recognized in Dusty. Independent and adventuresome, suntanned and self-assured, Rick could ask for directions in eight different languages and could understand the answer in five. They began meeting for coffee, then dinner, and finally at her apartment during Bryan's late nights at the hospital.

Expecting Rick, she hadn't thought twice about opening her door that night, and Bryan coming home early had been nothing but a strange and fortunate coincidence. If her attacker hadn't found his way into the building, if he'd chosen another victim, if Rick hadn't been in a fender-bender out of range of a cell tower, Bryan would have come home to an entirely different scenario.

Rick's messages accumulated on her cell phone, but she never returned his calls. There were too many ifs—if she hadn't opened the door, if Bryan hadn't come home, if Rick had arrived first. She dropped out of school, enrolling again after Rick had graduated.

Now she misses him. She misses being someone who can open doors without fear.

The next morning, she and Bryan oversleep. He grimaces as he swallows four aspirin. "Our last day in Africa," he says, "and I'm hung over."

They hurry to the Land Cruiser, where Victor is cleaning the windows. Everyone is there but Dusty, who arrives a few minutes later. "*Mambo,*" he says.

"*Poa,*" Victor replies, and Dana watches them exchange a complex handshake. In the daylight, Dusty's eyes are lighter, the faded gold of a lion's, the irises rimmed with dark brown.

The day simmers and boils over by the time they finish a picnic near a lagoon. Land Cruisers churn copper-colored dirt into the air, and as Dana stands, hoping for a breeze, she feels the dust settle on her face, in her teeth.

Later, as the sun begins to lower in the sky, they see a long line of vehicles gathered at the side of the road. Victor pulls over, just in front of a pair of Cape buffalo, younger and healthier than the pair at the lounge.

Dana doesn't notice the calf lying in the grass until Bakari points it out.

"And at eleven o'clock," he says, his finger stretching outward, "is a female lion in the grass. Her companion is at two o'clock."

Through her binoculars, Dana sees only the top of the female's head, the perk of her ears. Her coat is the precise color of the dry and faded grass, and she is completely still. Her mate, despite his larger head and the fluff of his mane, is nearly as invisible. Their heads are turned in the direction of the buffalo, but they don't appear terribly interested.

One of the buffalo is standing over the calf—this is the mother, Bakari says—and the other is an adolescent male, also hers. They've caught the scent of the lions, but they don't move.

One by one, the vehicles begin to pull away, and Victor brings them to a vacated spot right in front of the clearing. Soon they are the only ones left. After twenty minutes of silence, Jill says impatiently, "Nothing's happening."

"The lions have eaten recently," Bakari says, "but if there is a good opportunity, they will take it. And this baby doesn't look well."

Dana steps onto the seat and leans her forearms against the roof, giving herself a wide-angle view of the clearing, though she's not yet sure she wants one.

"Here it comes," Dusty says. He is so close to her she can feel his breath on her neck.

The male lion moves toward the buffalo, slowly and steadily, his focus unwavering. Dana takes in a breath. When she glances to the left, she sees that the female lion is now on her feet, although still far away.

She turns back just in time to see the male charge. He makes no sound except for the rustle of his body through the grass. The female buffalo charges back. Then they circle each other, not making contact, intent on circling, the adolescent buffalo close behind his mother and the calf now lurching unsteadily to its feet. The grunts of the buffalo and the lion's panting rise above the sigh of the grass under their feet.

Suddenly, the lion dodges the buffalo, then plunges forward and sinks his teeth into the baby's neck, holding tight and dragging the tiny body away even as the mother moans and begins to charge toward him. The instant she lowers her head, the lion releases his lock on the calf's throat and turns on her. His companion has arrived on the scene and stands guard over the dead calf as the male chases the two surviving buffalo toward the road.

Dana turns so fast that she hits her knee on the metal armrest of the seat in front of her. She watches the lion run the buffalo across the road, far into a meadow on the other side. A few moments later, the lion returns, panting heavily, his mouth falling open, baring teeth the size of Dana's fingers. His coat is bright gold in the setting sun.

The female stayed with the carcass; she has turned it over and is now licking its belly, preparing to gut it. The male stands over her, looking around, eyes passing over the Land Cruiser as if it were no more than a dead tree next to the road.

Dana's legs are trembling, her knee aching, and she sinks down into one of the seats. The car is silent. Finally Bakari says, "It's late. We have to get back. The park is already closed."

The sky is deepening behind the acacias, and theirs is the only car on the road. Victor drives faster than he ever has, and in the quiet it feels as if everyone is holding a collective breath. The vultures are silhouetted in the trees, waiting, motionless, against the purpling sky.

After the farewell dinner, Bryan asks to see Patrick's digital photos of the kill. Dana had forgotten about the camera; she hadn't taken a single photo.

"Give him the whole camera," Jill says. "I don't want to see them."

In the front of the lounge, a trio of young, bare-chested musicians is setting up. Dana's knee is swollen and throbbing, and she's grateful for the twinges of pain, for something to focus on. She had known, deep down, that the little calf didn't have a chance—but somehow she'd hoped that the laws of nature would change, just once, and that the weaker one could prevail.

One of the young men begins warming up on the drums. As Bryan looks at Patrick's photos, Dana lets her eyes drift over to Dusty. As she watches, he drains his glass. Then he stands and walks over to her, leaning down.

"I'm in number twelve," he says, close to her ear. Before she can respond, he adds, "Look at your watch. Tell me what time it is."

She raises her wrist. "Nine-thirty," she tells him.

"Okay, thanks." He straightens. "'Night, all."

Dana waits for a break in the conversation before telling Bryan, "I want to check out the gift shop before we leave. Do you want to come?"

"I've seen it, remember?" Bryan says. "You go ahead."

"I might head back after," she says. He fishes the key out of his vest.

At reception, a tall African in a hotel uniform stops her. "What is your bungalow number?" he says.

"Twelve," she says, slipping the key into her pocket.

"I'll walk you," he says. "Because of the buffalo. They have been up here at the pool, for water."

It's a bad omen, she thinks, but it's too late: he is already leading her down the torch-lit path. At Dusty's bungalow, her escort waits, and she explains, "My husband is already here," and knocks. She moves forward, trying to evade the slice of light falling across the entryway.

Dusty opens the door, wearing jeans and nothing else. His hair is combed back, dark and damp from a shower.

"He walked me home, because of the buffalo," she explains.

"Oh." Dusty roots through a pile of bills and change. He gives the man a handful of shillings. "*Asante.*"

"*Karibu.*"

Dusty shuts the door and leans against it, smiling.

"I don't know what I'm doing here," she says.

"Well, you can't leave now. Not with the buffalo roaming around."

She knows he's joking, but something inside her chest tightens.

Dusty takes her arm. "Come on," he says. "I got a bottle of whiskey in duty-free. I forgot to get ice, though."

"I don't want anything." She tugs her arm free. "I should go."

They are standing near a rickety armoire, and he moves closer. "Don't go," he says.

He puts his hands against the armoire, on either side of her head. When he leans in to kiss her, she whips her arms up and breaks out of the box he has put her in. Before he can turn around, she is across the room.

He stands where she left him. She looks at his bare chest, tanned and strong, and feels a sudden rush of desire and fear so closely mingled she doesn't know which might prevail. She takes a step forward. He is about six feet tall, she surmises. "How much do you weigh?" she asks.

He doesn't move. "About one-ninety. Why?"

A few more steps, and she is standing next to the bed. She yanks back the mosquito netting, untucking it from under the mattress and shoving it aside. She sits down and waits.

"Are you sure?" he asks.

She nods.

When he reaches the edge of the bed, she scoots backward, then lies down. She shudders, almost involuntarily, when she sees him above her. When he bends his head down, she is only vaguely aware of the pressure of his lips on hers. She lifts her arms above her head.

Within a few seconds, she has gone through the moves; he is on his back at the edge of the bed, and she's straddling him. This would be the time for her to drive her elbow into his solar plexus, to leap off him and escape. Instead, she eases him toward the middle of the bed. She leans down and kisses him, letting her hands trail down his chest to the waistband of his jeans.

She feels his hands on her face, her back, her thighs. He lifts his hips so she can pull off his jeans, but then he waits, letting her free her breasts from her bra and guide his hands there, then his mouth, and waiting as she takes off her khakis and lowers herself onto him. Only then does she give him permission to move, to sit up as she wraps her legs around his torso, to turn over, to flip yet again onto his back.

Afterward, as the fan swirls the hot air above them, she hears African music from the lounge, a mosquito singing in her ear. When she realizes where she is, what she's done, she sits up.

Dusty swings his legs over the side of the bed. "I'll walk you back."

"Are you crazy?"

"The buffalo," he says.

She quickly puts on her clothes, which stick to her damp skin. "I'd rather be gored by one of those buffalo than caught by Bryan."

He steps forward and gives her a long, lingering kiss. "You're afraid of all the wrong things," he tells her.

Along the path, torches flicker in the breeze, creating shadows. Every movement causes her to stop and scan the bushes along the path. But the buffalo are nowhere near.

Her bungalow is dark and quiet. She showers and gets into bed. Finally, Bryan returns. As he lies down next to her, she holds her breath.

But he drifts off, and again she waits for sleep. She is trying to sort out her thoughts when a noise outside interrupts, and she turns toward the window. She hears the eerie sounds of hyenas calling to one another in the distance, recognizing the high-pitched *rrr-oop!* that Bakari had once simulated for them. The cries come from all around, gradually coalescing, pinpointing a single direction.

Then, suddenly, it is silent. She listens tensely as Bryan sleeps beside her. After a few moments of almost preternatural stillness, she hears a loud groaning sound, like the mooing of cow, and the hyenas begin to laugh, voices rising in triumphant cackles, announcing a victory. After about five minutes, the laughter dies away, and she hears the distant but unmistakable yawning sigh of lions.

The others heard it, too. At breakfast, Bakari tells them what happened.

"One of the old buffalo wandered away from the lodge," he says. "The hyenas were able to overpower it."

Dana feels a sudden, sharp sorrow. "I thought I heard lions."

Bakari nods. "The lions came and took the carcass from the hyenas. But they only eat about a third of it, mostly the entrails, and leave the rest. So the hyenas will it finish off. Even the bones."

At the airport, Dusty leaves the group to check in for his flight to Dar es Salaam. Like the others, Dana shakes his hand, releasing it quickly. But later, after she hears his flight called, she wanders over to the window. She imagines his plane is the one straight ahead, that he is looking out his window, seeing her through the glass.

As the plane rises into the sky, she remembers leaving the paved drive of the lodge, looking over to the spot where she had first seen the two buffalo, searching for the survivor. She thought she was the only one looking until Dusty said, "There," and pointed. Then she saw it: the lone buffalo, standing between a pair of acacia trees. She noticed the graying of its coat, its wet nose, the flies gathered at the corners of its eyes, the way its body sloped forward, its head lower than its shoulders, in a posture of defeat. Its hooded eyes seemed to lock onto hers, deep brown and tired, as it lifted its head to watch her disappear.

NEVER TURN YOUR BACK ON THE OCEAN

We're in Turtle Town, just off the coast of Wailea, and Tanner's in the water, where I'd like to be. But Bryanna, his younger sister, is afraid of the ocean—of nearly everything, for that matter—so we lean over the rail of the boat, watching Tanner. I steal a wistful glance at the rocky outline of the coast.

When Tanner and Bryanna's parents asked me to come along to Maui, I thought I'd be in for some relaxation, not twenty-four-hour babysitting. After all, back in LA, I've been more a chauffeur than a nanny, picking the kids up from school and taking them to their guitar lessons or dance classes or surf camp or friends' houses. I took the job because it was easier than waiting tables at Sal's, and it left my mornings free for auditions. The kids' mother—an actress herself, and a successful one—even said she'd give me time off if I get a callback. Lately, though, I haven't had any callbacks. So I figured a trip to Hawai'i couldn't hurt, especially since it was entirely paid for by my employers, and they'd presumably be spending time together as a family while I basked on the beach. Instead, I've hardly seen the parents since we landed.

"Are you sure he can breathe okay?" Bryanna looks up at me, her forehead wrinkled. At eight, she has the worry lines of a fifty-year-old.

"Yes," I tell her, putting on a patient face. One thing this job has taught me, if not how to *be* patient, is how to *act* patient. My agent, Twig, always told me to find a day job that mirrors my chosen career, but I don't think this is exactly what she had in mind. "He's perfectly fine, Bree," I say.

Then we hear the screams.

I whip my head around. The shouting is coming from the other side of the boat, but I can't see anything. Turning back, I see that Tanner is below us, in plain view, alive and well, and when he lifts his head from the water, I motion him to the stepladder at the side of the boat. His eyes behind his mask look wide, surprised, his upper lip fat from the snorkel. I don't know what's happening, but I want Tanner out of the water. The screaming continues—a girl's voice, growing more hysterical by the second.

Uncharacteristically, Tanner obeys me. "Hurry up," Bree shrieks, and I put my hand on her shoulder. "He's fine, see?" I say, in a tone that blends reassurance and maternal comfort. I'm getting good at this.

When Tanner's safely on board, I steer them to a bench and sit them down. "Wait here. I'm going to see what's going on. Don't move, you promise?"

They both nod, too shaken to argue.

I rush aft and see two crew members hauling a skinny, bikini-clad girl out of the water. She looks about fourteen and is gasping for breath between sobs. I remember her from earlier, when we boarded. She refused to put on a wetsuit or a snorkel and mask. She dove prettily off the boat and tossed her hair around in the water as if she were doing a shampoo ad, reminding me of a woman I auditioned with a couple of weeks ago. The woman at the audition was nearly as scantily clad, and she couldn't stop flipping her hair. The way the casting director's eyes clung to her, I knew I didn't have a chance.

As I watch the girl being lifted from the water, I see huge red welts covering her body, snaking from her middle up to her arm, and fiery streaks across her neck and the right half of her face.

"I'm going to *die!*" the girl screams, flailing her good arm and her legs.

"Oh my God," her mother shrieks, clutching at one of the crew members. "Help her, help her!"

"She's okay," he tells her calmly. "Looks like she swam into a man-o-war. They're nasty, the sting hurts, but they're not deadly. She's going to be fine."

That's when the girl starts vomiting.

I turn away and head back to Bryanna and Tanner. They are sitting right where I left them.

"What is it?" Bree asks when I approach.

"Nothing," I say. "Just a girl who got stung by a man-o-war. She'll be all right."

"But she said she was going to *die*," Bree protests. "I heard her."

"People who say they're going to die usually don't."

Tanner looks anxiously out at the water. "Are there more out there?"

"Maybe," I say, though I have no idea, "but they can't get you in your wetsuit."

After the girl calms down, and after the Coast Guard comes to take her to the hospital, the crew tells us that anyone wearing a wetsuit can go back in. No one does.

As we disembark in Kihei, Bree says she forgot something and returns to the top deck. As she comes back down, I watch her. She stops to tap her heels against every second stair. She thinks no one notices. I don't say anything.

The large warning signs rise from Wailea's coastline as if they're native to the environment. Like sentinels guarding every access point to the beach, their rows of yellow diamonds alert swimmers and passersby of high surf, sharp coral, rip currents, jellyfish, man-o-war, criminal activity.

The criminal activity diamond is my favorite. It has a drawing of a stick figure sprawled on its back, with another stick figure towering over it, a spindly arm raised. Tanner and I laughed when we first saw it, but Bryanna was terrified by it and all the others. She insists that she won't go into the water the whole time we're on Maui.

"Some way to spend your vacation," says Tanner.

"Hush," I tell him. This comes out sharply. Sometimes I just get too tired to work on voices and gestures and expressions.

We're finishing a long walk on the path that winds along the shoreline—beaches and lava rocks on one side, a billion dollars' worth of resorts on the other. Tanner and Bree are cranky because their parents didn't arrive home before their bedtime last night; Tanner couldn't tell them about the man-o-war incident, and Bree couldn't get the comfort she was hoping for. I doubted their parents would be either attentive or comforting and was just as glad they didn't appear until after we were all in bed.

They hired me two months ago. Twig didn't like the commitment level—she wants me to be completely free for anything she might find—but I pointed out that to make what I'm making as a nanny I'd have to work double shifts at Sal's seven days a week. And this, I told her, would make me age even faster than I already have. At twenty-four, I'm ancient. Twig—her real name is Mary, but everyone calls her Twig because she's five-eight and weighs about a hundred pounds—claims she's optimistic about my career, but she has begun to take longer to return my calls, and lately she's had her assistant respond to my emails. And even though she says she wants me free for auditions, she hasn't been sending much my way. The last few casting calls I've gone to were ones I heard about at Sal's, where everyone's an actor. Sal's is a theme restaurant—its full name is Sal Manella's—where, as the slogan goes, *The food won't kill you but the service might.* The joke is that the wait staff snaps at all the customers in phony displays of surliness, but the real joke, I think, is that everyone's there because they can't find serious acting work, so the surliness gets more authentic all the time.

Landing the nanny job gave me a little hope, what with the kids' mother being an actress and their father a producer. I suppose I thought they might somehow pick up on my talents and give me my big break. But I don't see them very often, and when I do, it's like handing off a baton in a race—a brief moment of contact, and they're gone again.

The irony, of course, is that I *am* acting, every day. I'm a housewife who never got married, a mother who never got pregnant. I'm playing a role, but they don't give SAG memberships to nannies.

"What's this?" Tanner asks, squatting down on the path and pulling on a low grayish shrub with tiny white blooms.

"Don't touch," I say, and glance over at a plaque that lists the names of Hawai'i's native plants. "It's hinahina," I tell him. Everything needs to be educational when you're in the role of nanny. I'm not their teacher or their mother, but I pretend I'm both.

"And this?" He jumps up again and moves on, pointing at but not touching a large, leafy, sea-green plant that looks like sculpted rubber.

"Naupaka."

"How do you know all that?" he asks suspiciously, looking at me.

"I know everything."

"Yeah, *right*," he says, off and running again.

"Stay where I can see you," I call after him. My tone: caring yet authoritative.

From the coastal path, our resort comes into view. It looks spectacular, a whitewashed village rising from the mountainous folds of lava. From any angle, it's unlike anything I've ever seen. We're staying in a four-bedroom cottage with ocean views, a private wading pool, and lanais on three sides. Our cottage, I discovered, costs $2,500 a night, and it comes with the use of a Mercedes convertible. The parents drive this, and for me and the kids they've rented a Chevy Cavalier.

On the beach, hotel employees constantly cross the sand, pulling up lounge chairs, proffering trays of ice water and sliced pineapple. They're all young guys, all tanned and beautiful. One in particular catches my eye, a blond guy with cropped, sun-bleached hair. He is arranging a trio of lounge chairs, and the muscles in his arms ripple under smooth brown skin and that flaxen hair. It is tragic that they are required to wear shirts.

We return to the cottage to get changed, and I slather the kids in waterproof sunscreen. Back on the beach, the guy I was admiring asks if we'd like some chairs.

"Three, please," Tanner pipes up.

"You got it," the guy says. He lifts the chairs from a stack at the end of the beach and places them according to Tanner's instructions.

"Thank you," I say.

"My pleasure," he says, and smiles. "My name's Cody, if you need anything."

And I'm Karey, if *you* need anything, I want to say. But I only smile back, repeating his name to myself as we settle down. For the first time since we arrived, I feel as though there might be something here for me.

I manage to steal glances at Cody every once in a while. He reminds me of the surfers I see on the beaches in Malibu, the ones I am too intimidated to approach. People think being an actress means you're confident, outgoing, assertive. But I can only be these things when I'm performing. At Sal's, I could bark at customers and dance on their tables without a trace of self-consciousness. But when it's me, just Karey, wanting to exchange a few simple words with a hotel employee, I am paralyzed.

Lately, I have stopped telling people I meet that I'm an actress—they always want to know what I've been in. In my two years in LA, I've been offered only a small role in a pilot that never panned out and a nonspeaking walk-on role in an episode of *Scrubs*. I was on camera so briefly that even my mother didn't see me; she taped the show and had to watch it again just to spot me. Twig has told me that I should consider soap operas. It's steady work, she says, and with my looks—not tall enough, not skinny enough, a redhead with the wrong skin tone to get away with going blonde—I can't count on landing any starring film roles. One of the big ironies of the industry—aside from the catch-22 of needing a SAG card to get a film role and not being eligible for SAG membership until you've done a film—is that in order to have the body of a film star, you need the kind of money you can only make by starring in a film.

It doesn't matter anyhow: Cody doesn't look my way. So mostly I keep my eyes on Tanner, who has rented a boogie board and charged it to the cottage. Bree sits on a lounge chair next to me with the latest Harry Potter. She's hunched over the book, knees up, in her yellow plastic sunglasses, red-and-white Hawai'ian-print hat, and blue tankini. She tugs on her sunhat, twice on both sides and once in the front. As anxious as I've been these days, when I look at Bree, I feel strangely sad and protective.

I often wonder whether people mistake me for Tanner and Bree's mother, or perhaps an older sister. It's possible in LA, where everyone looks about twenty-five. But I know another nanny would never make such a mistake; we always recognize one another. I can always tell a nanny from a parent because nannies are careful, as if they're being watched. And I can tell because I've never seen a nanny ignore a child the way a parent might, probably because it would be too much like napping on the job. I've watched parents talk over and around their screaming children, but we nannies don't have that luxury.

The kids are tired by sunset, so I order dinner from room service. They deliver a flatbread pizza, a huge Caesar salad, a hamburger and fries, and a bottle of red wine. I pour glasses of milk from the fridge for

Tanner and Bree and pour myself a very full glass of wine.

We sit in the dining area off the kitchen. I put some salad next to Tanner's hamburger and watch as Bree cuts her pizza into eight small, even pieces. Just before putting them into her mouth, she cuts each one in half. She chews each mouthful twelve times, even if by then there's nothing left to chew.

My own bite of salad has turned to mush in my mouth, and I wash it down with a generous swallow of wine. I chew my mouthfuls only eight times, but this is because I take smaller bites. As I watch Bree, I move salad around on my plate; I can't eat my own food while watching her or I lose count.

Has she always done this? I ask myself. It took me weeks to notice her rituals, and only now do I find myself wondering whether she invented them herself or whether she picked them up from me. I don't think she did, though. She is the same kind of child I was—nervous, edgy, shrill—but her rituals are different, neater, like her background. She has grown up with affluence, two parents, a sibling, while I had an unemployed mother, no father (I don't count her on-and-off boyfriends as family), one pet gerbil, and no money to speak of. But I imagine my rituals started when I was about Bree's age. Gradually, mine became messier—even involving sharp-edged objects—not that anyone paid enough attention to detect the damage. But I could hardly show up at auditions with scratches all over my arms or fingernails bitten down to the quick. So I've watched the scars fade, and I keep my hands neatly manicured for their own protection. It was acting that saved me, and I think it still saves me a little bit every day.

After dinner, I load everything onto the tray again and leave it outside the front door. We sit in the living room, where Tanner turns on the television and Bree opens her book. I pull out my new head shots. I've brought them with me because I need to choose one; Twig is waiting for me to decide so she can send it out. I flip through them, gazing at myself sitting on a stool, on the floor, leaning over, leaning back, hands cupping my face, my neck. Nothing looks natural to me. In an attempt to avoid the creases produced by smiling, I'm straight-mouthed, almost lifeless.

"What's this?" Tanner asks, squatting next to me on the couch, pushing his head in front of mine.

"Head shots," I tell him. "Help me choose?"

He looks at them thoughtfully for a few moments. "This one," he says finally, pointing.

"Why?" I study the one he's picked. My head is tilted, eyes slightly narrowed. It's the only one that hints of a smile; I'd set it aside because I didn't want anyone to mistake the dimples for wrinkles.

"It looks the most like you." He jumps up and sits down again in front of the TV.

As Tanner watches the end of his show, I call Twig's cell phone. I get her voice mail and leave a message, asking her to call me back. Then I hang up and announce bedtime. Tanner and Bree both protest. They haven't seen their parents all day.

"Come on, I'll tuck you in," I say. They follow me down the hall. I stand in the doorway as they brush their teeth. My eyes are on Bree, the rhythm of her brushing, the precision of her spitting and rinsing.

When I pull the covers up to her chin, she reaches up and hugs me. She's never done this before. I hug her back and tell her to have sweet dreams. Without a script, I'm not sure what else to say.

Tanner asks me if I'm going to hang out with his parents. "I don't know," I say.

"Tell them about the man-o-war," he says.

"I'll try."

It's past ten o'clock when the parents get home, both of them checking messages on their cell phones as they walk in the door.

I stand up. They don't seem to notice me. "I think I'll go for a drive," I say. I hesitate for a moment, hoping one of them will toss me the keys and say, *Why don't you take the Mercedes tonight?* But they're both returning calls, so I grab the keys to the Chevy.

When I enter the parking lot, I'm watching my feet move below me, over and around the cracks. The squeal of tires stopping short jars me, and I look up to see Cody at the wheel of a dirty Jeep. He pokes his head out the window.

"You should watch where you're going," he says. "I almost hit you. The lighting's so bad around here."

"Mood lighting," I say, "for the honeymooners." Flirtatious tone, cool delivery, despite the fact that my heart rate is accelerating.

"Yeah, that's what the brochures say. Even our parking lots are romantic."

"You're Cody, right?" I say, as if I'd forgotten.

He nods. "You're the one with the kids, on the beach."

"They're not my kids."

"I know that." A car pulls up behind him and flashes its lights, and Cody glances in the rearview mirror. "So do you have the night off?"

I nod, and he says, "I'm meeting some people in Kihei. Want to come?"

I walk around to the passenger's side and get in. He drives out of the parking lot and down the road, toward the luxury shopping center. When he stops at the light, I say, "I'm Karey."

He offers his hand, which I think is sweet in an old-fashioned sort of way. Then he leans his head back on the headrest. "I'm always so glad to get out of there. It's like being on another planet." He turns to look at me. "You look like you haven't been back in the real world for a long time yourself," he says.

We stop at his apartment so he can change. It's a tiny furnished studio off South Kihei Road with a tiled floor and a moldy smell. Beach towels hang from his lanai, and a surfboard leans against a wall near the galley kitchen. Cody takes off his work shirt, the one with the hotel logo, then roots around in a duffel bag for another. I stare at his tanned, slender back, but when he turns around, I pretend to be looking out the window.

"Ready?" he asks. He doesn't change out of his swim trunks.

Inside the bar, surfboards cover the ceiling, and sawdust covers the floor. The music of a reggae band pulses from a small stage in the corner, and the rest of the room is crowded with the splayed arms and legs of chairs, tables, and drunken surfers.

Cody buys me a beer and introduces me to his friends, three guys in their mid-twenties with bedraggled, sun-bleached hair and goatees, and a woman with long brown dreadlocks. They're here to work and surf, surf and work—they do year-round what Cody is doing for the summer. He just graduated from college, he told me in the car. I didn't want to tell him that I'm an actress, and he never asked, but for some reason, as we walked to the bar, I just said it. He said, *Cool.* That was it.

"So what's next for you?" I ask him when we have a moment alone.

He shrugs and says, "Who knows?"

"Doesn't that worry you?"

"Nah. I'll go back to the mainland in a few months, see what's up, and if nothing's going on, I'll just come back. I'm stokin' on the waves here."

"Well, what's not to like?" I ask, glancing around at the half-naked, suntanned crowd that seems to sway as one to the music. "But don't you have goals, for a career or something?"

"What's the rush?"

"Old age," I say, suddenly feeling confessional. "I'm getting farther from being an actress every minute I'm not out there. My agent isn't calling me back like she used to, and that's very bad news. No one ever actually says *no* in Hollywood, you know; they just stop returning your calls, but that's—"

"Whoa," he says. "Slow down. Are you this intense about everything?"

"Are you this laid back about everything?"

Cody only smiles and makes the *shaka* sign with hand. Then his friends are back, arms full of beer bottles, and our conversation drifts away.

Later I follow them all to the beach. I watch from the sand as they bodysurf by the light of the moon and of cars passing along South Kihei Road. Under the moonlight, their bodies framed in the glare of headlights, they look like pale sea creatures, shoulders angular and smooth, hair wet and slick against their necks and faces.

Cody is the last one out of the water, and we're alone on the beach. He shivers a couple of times in the night air, but I don't touch him, as much as I want to. He puts on his T-shirt, which sticks to his chest. As we walk along the beach, toward his apartment, he kisses me, and his mouth is as relaxed and smooth and easy as the rest of him. Despite the wiry muscles I feel in his arms, his back, I sense not a single ripple of tension. I want to absorb him, to take all this calm away with me.

But I have to get back. He drops me off at the employees' entrance at the resort.

"See you," he says.

I watch him drive away, and then stand there, staring into the darkness of the road and listening to the rush of the sea behind me.

✧

I see Cody on the beach the next day, but I only have time to smile and wave; Tanner and Bree are arguing over the lounge chairs because one has a tear in it.

"I'll take that one," I tell them and lay out my towel across its back. "No more fighting."

Tanner drops his towel and runs straight into the water. He didn't rent a boogie board this morning, and Bree won't take her eyes off him.

"The sea looks angry today," she says.

"It's fine, Bree," I say. Frustration creeps into my voice; I'm not paying attention. Twig never called me back. I wish I hadn't told Cody I'm an actress. I have a sudden need for all my failures to be private.

I tell Bree I'm watching Tanner, but she keeps looking up from her book; she can't help it. She tugs on her hat. Twice on the sides, once in the front. Repeat.

Since she's got such a close eye on her brother, I allow myself a glance at Cody. I see him about twenty yards away, talking with a young couple, smiling as the woman hands him a tip. He walks back to the entrance to the beach, slipping the money into a pocket of his trunks. I follow him with my eyes, but he doesn't look back. I raise a hand to my mouth, itching to bite my nails, then lower it again and begin to twist one of my rings around my finger, five times clockwise, then five times back. I repeat it until I feel calmer.

Tanner runs up to us, breathless, shaking water from his hair.

"You should be more careful," Bree says. "The waves are rough today. Didn't you see the sign?"

"How could I miss it?"

"It says, 'Never turn your back on the ocean.' You keep doing that," Bree tells him.

"Well, how am I supposed to body surf?" He raises his arms over his head and hunches over, lurching toward her. "What's it gonna do, gobble me up?" He's dripping saltwater onto the crisp pages of her book.

"Hey!" she complains.

And I'm thinking of Twig, wondering whether she'll ever call me back, realizing that it's probably true—that you can't turn your back for a moment without getting swallowed up, or sucked under.

"Chill," Tanner says, dropping his arms and flopping down in the sand. I see a honeybee swirl around his head. "Careful," I say. "There's a bee."

Bree lets out a shriek, and Tanner jumps up. He sees the bee hovering near the ground and begins kicking sand over it.

"Tanner, don't." I grab his arm. I kneel down in the sand and see a flutter of tiny wings under the grains. I take Bree's bookmark and gently unearth the bee. It crawls around for a moment or two, dazed, then unsteadily rises into the air and flies away.

"You didn't have to do that," I say. "It didn't do anything to you."

"It could've stung me," he protests.

"So? You'd live."

He pouts for a couple minutes. For a reason I don't understand, I want to teach them to be good, to do no harm.

Then he stands and pulls off Bree's hat. "Come in the water," he says.

"No," she says. "I'm reading."

"You're such a chicken." He tosses the hat back.

Bree puts it on and does her tugging. Tanner sprints for the water again. I watch as he swims out to a group of kids on boogie boards, until a gust of wind flips my towel over the right half of my face. I pull the towel away and turn to drape it back over the lounge chair, and when I look back at the water, Tanner is gone.

My heart leaps into my throat, and for a moment I can't move. Then I glimpse him briefly, head and flailing arms bursting from the surface of the water before the current drags him under again. By the time I struggle to my feet, Bree is already up, running into the sea. The sight of that jolts me into action. I run after her.

She's in up to her thighs, screaming out to Tanner. "Swim parallel to the shore," she cries, waving her arm to the south. "Swim parallel to the shore!"

She watches anxiously, reaching for her hat, which has blown off her head and is floating nearby. She tugs at the air around her ears instead, unaware of what she's doing.

For an instant, Tanner's head bobs up again, and this time both Bree and I wave our arms. "Parallel!" she screams again. I twirl my ring, five times around, five back, five around, five back.

Tanner seems to be moving south, seems to be getting out from under the riptide's grip. Then he is swimming in toward us, slower than usual, his energy sapped. I start toward him, but a tall man with wet gray hair is already at his side, holding him by the arm until both his feet are steady on the sand. Bree and I help lead him back to the beach. I see Bree's hat and scoop it out of the water.

"*Thank* you," I tell the man, once we're back on the sand.

"Sure thing," he says. "Amazing they don't have lifeguards here, for what we're paying." He nods toward Bree. "You did great, kiddo," he tells her. "You've got a good head on your shoulders."

She doesn't seem to hear him, and I look over to see Cody beside us. "What happened?" he asks, looking from Tanner to Bree to me.

"Riptide," I say. "I think he's all right." But I am shaking so badly I can hardly stand up. Even Bree seems calmer than I feel.

"Let's sit him down," Cody says. Back at our chairs, he kneels in the sand in front of Tanner. "You okay?"

Tanner nods. He's coughing and spits onto the sand. "Swallowed water," he croaks out.

"I've swallowed gallons in my lifetime," Cody says. "It doesn't taste too good, but it won't kill you." He smiles and runs his hands over Tanner's shoulders, arms, and legs. "Anything hurt?" he says. "Anything feel weird?"

Tanner shakes his head. Cody looks closely at Tanner's eyes and asks him to follow his finger as he moves it in front of his face, right and left, up and down. I remember him telling me he'd been a lifeguard as a teenager in San Diego. "Did you get turned around underwater, hit your head on the sand?" he asks.

"No."

"Okay." Cody stands up and says to me, "I think he'll be okay. You could take him to see a doctor, just in case, but I wouldn't worry."

"Are you sure?"

He nods. I look away from his face and take a deep shuddering breath. I feel his hand touch the back of my head for a second before he leans down again. "Take it easy the rest of the day, okay?" he tells Tanner. "Maybe you can hang by the pool instead."

To my surprise, Tanner agrees. "Happy, Bree?" he says, peering at her through sea-reddened eyes. She hits him on the shoulder. "Jerk," she mutters.

Then they're arguing again and Cody is gone and I turn and see families and kids in the water, and for a brief moment it's as if nothing had happened.

But it did happen. One of these children almost drowned in my care.

We're at the pool. Bree is back to forgoing the water, and Tanner is back to his usual self, hurtling down the slide and joining a game of water volleyball. I'm afraid to take my eyes off him.

I spin my ring, remembering when I first took this job, when all I thought was that it would be easier and pay better than waitressing. The parents had contacted my references and done background checks, but still—I don't think I once made sure the kids wore seatbelts when I drove them or waited until they were safely inside the door at a friend's house when I dropped them off. And now, in the heavy heat of the afternoon, the sudden weight of my responsibility seems to freeze the air in my chest.

I'm relieved when the sun begins slip to away and it's time to leave the pool. We don't talk about the riptide over dinner, and the kids are quieter than usual. We're watching television when the parents come home. Neither Tanner nor Bree mentions what happened, and I don't either, not even after the kids are in bed. I know I should, even though Tanner's okay, but I can't bring myself to do it.

I leave them together at the cottage and set out for a walk. It's dark now, the resort's walkways lit by the flicker of tiki torches. I head down to the beach, to the coastal walk, ignoring the warning signs and pushing through the gate. A bright security light comes on, but a moment later it shuts off. The glow from the resorts is enough to allow me to see, and I walk slowly along the path. The roar of the surf seems even louder in the dark, and a breeze carries sea spray to my face. I walk for a long time, thinking of what will happen when I return to LA, of what will happen when Twig stops returning my calls for good. What scares me more than losing Twig is the knowledge that I'll have to keep this job, this responsibility; I'll have to make my performance real. I chew at a couple of fingernails.

When I return to the resort, I find Cody and another of the hotel employees on the beach, stacking chairs by the light of the tiki torches. I offer to help. They don't let me, so I stand there while they work.

"I think my agent is dumping me," I tell him. I feel he's the only person, besides the kids, who won't find the news depressing or pathetic.

"Oh," he says. "Sorry to hear that." He looks up. "What does it mean?"

"I guess I'll have to find a new one. Start over."

"That's not always such a bad thing, catching the next wave." He wedges the last chair into place and asks if I want to go for a drive. I say okay.

We go to Big Beach, which I'd read about but hadn't taken the kids to—it's the roughest beach in Wailea, with waves coming in at six to ten feet even on a calm day. In the parking lot, Cody takes a blanket and a flashlight from the Jeep.

On the beach, we struggle to spread the blanket in the wind, but it's so dark that it's hard to see, and we end up sitting on one edge of it, our feet in the sand. Cody puts his arm around me, and we look up at the sky, a rich velvety black, studded with stars. I can't see the waves, but I can hear their power: silence, then a rush, a pause, and a thrumming crash, the cycle repeating itself over and over again, like Bree's rituals. Like my own.

Another wave crashes, and in the silence that follows, Cody murmurs, "That was a big one. Twelve-footer, probably. Imagine being out there."

"Never turn your back on the ocean," I say.

I feel him shake his head. "Nah. If you know it well enough, you're not turning your back on it. You're becoming a part of it."

"Spoken like a true surfer." I laugh.

He stands up. My shoulders cool without the warmth of his arm.

"Where are you going?"

"For a swim," he says.

"Are you crazy? You'll drown out there." I strain to see his face, but he's only a vague shape in front of me. I see him move, and then his shirt lands next to me on the blanket.

"Coming in?" he says.

I sit for a moment, completely still. Then I stand up and brush the sand off my legs. I follow the sound of his voice in the dark, lost in the surprising calm of an unrehearsed moment.

ACKNOWLEDGMENTS

Thanks to Rebecca Raymond, for being my Tongan guidebook and dictionary, and to John Yunker, for reading every word.

And thanks to the editors of the publications in which the following stories first appeared, in slightly different form:

"First Sunday": *Indiana Review*
"Translation Memory": *Bellevue Literary Review*
"The Ecstatic Cry": *The Ontario Review*
"The Road to Hana" (as "Twin Falls"): *American Literary Review*
"Forgetting English": *new south* (formerly *gsu review*)
"Never Turn Your Back on the Ocean": *Roanoke Review*

Photo: Matt Janecek

Midge Raymond's award-winning stories have appeared in the *American Literary Review*, the *Indiana Review*, the *Ontario Review*, the *Bellevue Literary Review*, the *North American Review*, the *Los Angeles Times*, and other publications. She currently lives in Seattle along with her husband and a fat orange cat. Visit her Web site at *www.ForgettingEnglish.com*.